D0723433

◆ KING ◆ PACHUCO ◆ AND ◆ PRINCESS MIRASOL

BY BONNIE K. RUCOBO

Author photograph by William Pearson
Cover design by Charlie Kenesson
Book design by Charlie Kenesson
Printed by Sheridan Books, Inc.
Wildflower Press colophon designed by Sherri Holtke

Library of Congress Control Number 2011927616

ISBN 978-0-9779933-6-9

 The Wildflower Press
P. O. Box 4757
Albuquerque, New Mexico 87196-4757
www.thewildflowerpress.com

Acknowledgments

Many writers and friends supported the creation of *King Pachuco and Princess Mirasol.* Among these were my writing coach Lucia Zimmitti who taught me to appreciate the form of the middle-grade novel, and Jeanne Shannon who edited the book and agreed to publish it under The Wildflower Press Imprint. Poets Annmarie Pearson, Elaine Schwartz, and Hilda Wales reviewed the copy. Poet and surgeon Sylvia Ramos read the manuscript with attention to its Spanish content. Albuquerque wood sculptor Paula Dimit reviewed the manuscript as well as did Sheryl De Jonge-Loavenbruck.

My friends Virginia Denton, Joanne Hageman, and Regina Speer also read the manuscript and supported me as I worked on it. Many thanks to William Pearson for taking the photograph of me and the "real" Pachuco which appears on the back cover.

Finally, I wish to thank my mother and sister for their assistance and encouragement as I completed my first children's novel.

Dedication

King Pachuco and Princess Mirasol is dedicated to my grandchildren and great-grandchildren, especially my granddaughter Maya Mariah who observed the bird cages in my kitchen in Albuquerque one morning and said, "Pachuco, you are the King, and Mirasol, you are the Princess."

And that is how the story began.

Contents

CHAPTER ONE

Princess Mirasol

Princess Mirasol, fair and petite, sat at the loom tossing her shiny, black ringlets as she expertly set the warp. It was a beautiful spring day, and she could smell the scent of cut grass and jasmine wafting in from the open windows in the sewing room. She wanted to be outside running through meadows of wildflowers or searching for creatures in tide pools along her Kingdom's many beaches. Anywhere but sitting at the loom.

Mirasol lived in the Kingdom of Pacifista, a planet in the next galaxy that whirled around its axis in a northeasterly direction from the Milky Way. Scientists on Earth had not yet discovered Pacifista, though there were many similarities between the two planets. Both had bountiful supplies of oxygen and hydrogen that created water in abundance and supported human life. Both contained essentially the same elements in their periodic tables.

But that is where the similarities ended. Life in Pacifista was peaceful. The citizens of Pacifista enjoyed lives of prosperity and peace. There was no poverty; no one ever went to bed hungry.

Citizens took great pride in one aspect of Pacifista. Every evening before sunset, rainbows filled the sky. These were no ordinary rainbows. They included breathtaking colors beyond the broad band of the Earth's visible spectrum. Pacifista's rainbows were like looking through a kaleidoscope that broke up color into complex and never-before-seen combinations. Every thirty to forty seconds the kaleidoscope shifted and created even more spectacular tones.

If you asked Mirasol, an eleven-year-old Princess, whether she was content with her life in Pacifista, she would respond, "Yes, for the most part." She lived in a small castle, as castles go, with her 80-year-old grandmother. She had never traveled more than twenty miles from home. Nor did she know anyone who had.

Mirasol's castle was not far from the immense Palace of King Pachuco, the location of all major festivities in the Kingdom. Her three older sisters had married and gone to live with their husbands' families. Her parents had passed away when a mysterious disease swept over the land. Mirasol was two years old when her parents died, and she went to live with her grandmother.

Mirasol's grandmother, Lupita, was short and plump with white hair that streamed down her back. She traveled to the local market weekly to sell produce from their garden. This morning as she was taking a wagonload of melons for sale, she told her granddaughter, "Mirasol, I hope that these melons fetch a good price. They are perfectly ripe and sweet. Maybe the King's buyer will purchase them.

"While I'm gone I want you to finish your dress for the King's ball," she instructed. "Remember you only have one week before the ball. Don't leave the castle this afternoon. Stay here and work on that dress."

Mirasol gave her a glum look but knew better than to protest. "Yes, Grandmother," she said.

She had worked on the dress for less than a half hour when Estella, her best friend, rang the clamorous bell at the castle entrance. Startled, Mirasol got up from her weaving and went to the door.

"I'm going fishing," said Estella. "Would you like to come?"

"I certainly would," Mirasol replied, "except that I've promised my grandmother I'd work on my dress for the ball." Her voice dropped as she pouted.

"Don't worry," said Estella. "We'll go to the lake now and be back with tonight's dinner before your grandmother returns."

Mirasol glanced between her loom and fishing rod. Then she picked up the fishing rod and followed her friend out the castle door and over the moat. The two headed toward the lake, a thirty-minute walk. When they reached the clear blue lake surrounded by twenty-foot pines, Mirasol removed her shoes and waded into the water before casting her line.

The catfish were biting. Mirasol hooked two large ones and Estella, an expert at fishing, caught four. Estella wanted to stay and take in the sun while Mirasol looked for unusual pebbles or studied wildlife, but Mirasol reminded her that if her grandmother knew of her whereabouts there would be a penalty to pay. "I'm sorry, Estella," she said, "but I've got to head back."

Estella accompanied her back to her castle, as it was on her way home. When they arrived, they saw Lupita's wagon hitched to the back of the castle. Lupita herself was standing at the castle doorway, hands on her hips.

"Why did you disobey me?" she asked her granddaughter gruffly. "Didn't I tell you not to leave the castle?"

"Y-Yes," Mirasol stammered. "I did start on the weaving, and we caught fish for dinner."

"You have not listened to me," said the grandmother, clearly annoyed. "Now you will stay in the castle until the King's ball, and I will be here with you to make sure you listen this time."

In other circumstances, Lupita and Mirasol would have invited Estella to join them for dinner. Estella lived in a tiny castle over the next hill with seven brothers and sisters. Often the family did not have meat or fish to eat, and they would ask Estella to join them for dinner whenever possible. But Mirasol knew that Lupita would not welcome a guest tonight, so she bade her friend farewell.

Even tasting the catfish fried to perfection with fresh herbs, onions, and potatoes did little to erase the sting of her grandmother's reprimand. Mirasol tried to obey her grandmother, but somehow things did not always go as she intended.

"You are eleven years old now, Mirasol," said Lupita after dinner. "Next week you will attend your first Royal Ball. In a few years we will find you a suitable husband. Look at your sisters. They are all married, and they are happy."

"I am not my sisters. I want to study wildlife. I want to have adventures…" Mirasol's voice trailed off.

"Now you sound like your father, always hiking and jotting notes about nature in notebooks," said Lupita. "This kind of thinking will get you nowhere," the grandmother snorted with disgust. "Tomorrow it's back to the loom and finishing your dress for the ball. And don't go snooping around the castle searching for your father's writings. They were destroyed years ago."

Mirasol was startled. She had no memories of her father and only knew him from a portrait on the wall in the castle entrance. She had not understood that her deep interest in the natural world stemmed in some way from him. A yearning to know more about her parents suddenly overwhelmed her; she felt flushed. She needed to know where and how they had lived and what had been important to them.

That night after her grandmother had retired, Mirasol searched through the books that lined the castle library shelves for her father's books about the natural world on Pacifista. Her grandmother had said they had been destroyed, but she had a hunch they still existed. Somewhere.

She was about to give up and go to bed when she saw a recessed wooden cabinet that was barely visible. The cabinet was locked, but she managed to pry open the door with a crowbar and a knitting needle. There at the bottom of the cabinet were nine handwritten notebooks containing drawings and commentary on the plants, animals, and insects of Pacifista.

"These must be my father's books!" exclaimed Mirasol as she began to pore over the volumes. She skimmed the first of the handwritten notebooks. Her spine tingled when she saw her father's handwriting and sketches. She found his notes about Pacifista's flora and fauna to be detailed and accurate based on her own observations. Some of them resembled the journals and sketches that she often prepared on her hikes outside the castle walls.

Her grandmother and even Fargo, the gnome-like maintenance man who had worked for her grandmother as long as she could remember, must have been aware that these books existed. She was overjoyed to have stumbled upon them. She wondered if her father had been a scientist or if observing the natural world had been a hobby, as it was hers.

She read through several volumes of her father's notebooks. She particularly enjoyed her father's description of the Kingdom's colorful bird population as "dense and thriving, especially in Pacifista's belt of rain forests." She was so caught up in her discovery that she completely lost track of time. Her father had seemed so distant from her; now she realized that he had always been closer than she knew.

It was almost morning when she returned the books to the shelves and headed for bed. She removed her shoes and crept stealthily past her grandmother's bedroom door. Listening at the keyhole, she heard Lupita's regular snoring. Smiling, she reached her bed and swiftly drifted off to sleep.

Early the next morning Lupita made sure that Mirasol returned to weaving the material for her ball dress. The dress was pure white with layers of lace and flower embroidery. The bodice was fitted; the sleeves were bouffant. The skirt reached the floor, almost hiding her white leather boots that buttoned up the side. She had been working on the outfit for more than a year.

When Mirasol finished weaving the material, her grandmother cut the fabric and pinned the dress's side seams. Then she stitched them by hand while Mirasol put the finishing touches on a cap that she planned to surround with a garland of fragrant gardenias on the night of the ball. She also began weaving the silk gloves that would extend past her elbows and match the rest of her ensemble.

"Grandmother," asked Mirasol as she wove, "how it is that my father was so interested in the natural world? Did you take him hiking on the nature trails in Pacifista? Did he make sketches of the animals and birds the way I do?"

"Mirasol, you know that I am not bothered by your chatter," she told her granddaughter, "but I have told you many times that a great deal of conversation is not allowed at Court. You have to learn how to hold your tongue. That is why I make you sit for an hour every morning without speaking a word."

Mirasol hated what she called these "periods of enforced silence," and sometimes hummed a folk song under her breath which Lupita did not notice as she was losing her hearing.

Living with her aging grandmother had required Mirasol to mature faster than most girls on Pacifista. Though her grandmother worked in the garden and cooked, she and Fargo performed much of the maintenance work at the castle. Mirasol also helped with the spinning, sewing, and weaving.

Lupita did not volunteer information about Mirasol's parents' lives. Her attitude suggested to Mirasol that it was too painful for her grandmother to talk about her parents or their untimely death.

"After lunch we have another run through of your Court etiquette drills," announced the grandmother. "You must be ready to show off your skills at the ball."

Lupita had taught Mirasol how to be gracious, when and how to curtsy, how to prepare her dance card, and how to manipulate the weighty silverware for the multiple course late-night dinner following the dance. She had practiced these motions over and over until they had become second nature.

Mirasol had learned the royal etiquette, but not without grumbling under her breath, "Why do I have to learn etiquette when I'd much rather be running through the woods of Pacifista?"

But only rarely did she voice her objections to her grandmother who would raise one eyebrow and say, "Mirasol, you must learn to appreciate your place in royal society. After all, you are not at the height of Pacifista royalty, but on a moderate level. You must learn what your status requires and take advantage of it whenever possible."

Mirasol did delight in one aspect of the preparation for the ball. She loved all kinds of dance: waltzes, minuets, polkas, and the Pacifista folk dances that she had been practicing since she was a young girl. She was so excited about trying out all the new dance steps at the King's ball that she danced for five hours every day.

Finally Lupita could stand it no longer. "Mirasol," she said, "you must rest and save your energy for the big night. I am getting winded just watching you whirl nonstop."

Though finishing Mirasol's ball gown occupied their time for the moment, Lupita and Mirasol also wove tapestries and sewed quilts when they had time. Their tapestries wound from room to room in their castle providing insulation from the winter cold and damp. They depicted Pacifista's exquisite rainbows, each radiating brighter and more vivid colors than the last. The grandmother and granddaughter never completed this tapestry but continued to add rainbows to cover the castle's stone walls that remained bare.

They also spent hours quilting with swatches of material that they arranged in squares in the most intricate patterns. They used a large wooden hoop to keep the three layers of quilting material in place as they sewed running stitches to hold the quilt top, the cotton batting, and the backing together.

Mirasol's and Lupita's castle had colorful quilts peeking out of closets, under beds, and overflowing from trunks scattered in various rooms. Mirasol's trunk that held the finery she planned to take with her when she married contained several elegant flowered quilts.

Finally, the day before the ball, the pair finished work on Mirasol's outfit. The dress fit Mirasol's small figure like a glove and transformed her into a glamorous and sophisticated young girl.

"You will be the most beautiful new face in the Court, without question," pronounced Lupita. "I predict that your Court debut will be a spectacular success."

Mirasol glowed when she heard her grandmother's praise. It was not often that she basked in her grandmother's approval.

"I have prepared a special dinner to celebrate our finishing your dress. I've bought some clams for the wonderful chowder that you like," she said, "and I'll put some fresh artisan bread into the oven to bake. We should eat in about an hour."

Mirasol's mouth was watering already. Clam chowder with fresh bread was her favorite meal, and she was hungry after weaving and having fittings of her dress all afternoon. "Let me help you set up for dinner," she offered. The woman and child, one old and stooped, and the other, with a definite spring to her step, headed toward the kitchen.

Within an hour the clam chowder was bubbling on the stove, and the bread was brown and crusty and out of the oven on cooling racks. The aroma of the food was delightfully enticing.

Lupita called her granddaughter to the table. "Eat while everything is hot," she commanded, ladling the thick soup into their wooden bowls. Then she sliced a loaf of the hearty bread and distributed pieces to herself and Mirasol.

While Mirasol prepared for bed that night, she couldn't help thinking about the Royal Ball. Though she had never been particularly excited about attending, now that the ball was hours away, her stomach was tight and her hands damp. She wondered if she would be able to sleep through the night.

What would the children of the Royal Court be like? Would she make friends and get to try out all her new dance steps? Would she have the most beautiful new face in the Court, as her grandmother predicted?

Maybe she would even meet the King, a boy just a year older than herself.

CHAPTER TWO

King Pachuco

P achuco was warily eying the three boards he had to break by hand. They were part of his trial for a black belt in the martial arts. The first, a flimsy piece of plywood, he split easily.

The second board, a plank four inches thick, looked daunting as he took his stance, breathed deeply, and focused. His hand came down heavily on the board. It creaked but failed to break. His hand felt numb, and after a few seconds was tender and throbbing. Beads of perspiration lined his forehead and the back of his neck.

Despite his failure to shatter the second board, he moved on to the third. He took his stance again and focused on the final board, ten inches thick. His palms were sweaty and his jaw clenched. Though he put all his effort into breaking the board, this one barely moved when he struck it. His hand was red and raw.

Pachuco at twelve years old was the youngest King in the history of Pacifista.

He was not used to failing any endeavor he set his mind to.

He was red-faced and sheepish when he turned towards the coach after the trial. His voice cracked as he told his mentor, a small but powerfully built man with a walrus mustache, "I knew I wasn't ready."

Pachuco's black hair cascaded down his back as he tossed his head. He was approaching five feet five inches in height, and his voice had already lowered from a bright falsetto to an unsettled bass.

The test for the black belt in the martial arts consisted of ten exercises, each increasing in complexity and requiring more agility and strength. Pachuco had succeeded in performing the first seven exercises. The first six were energy-generating postures that he was required to hold for twenty minutes each.

The seventh required that he remain stationary as his coach ran toward him head on. Seconds before the coach reached him, Pachuco was able to use his coach's momentum to throw him to the ground. Though Pachuco had performed this exercise many times, he could tell his mentor was giving it his all this morning and almost succeeded in pinning him.

How could he have failed the trial, he wondered. He had been practicing the martial arts for years, and just last week had successfully completed a preliminary test. This was the day of the Palace Ball, but that could not be the reason he was unsettled enough to flub the test.

"Nothing is lost," said the coach calmly. "Haven't you been working on your basic skills?"

Pachuco stomped out of the martial arts practice room. Why was his coach so matter-of-fact about his failing the battery of tests for the black belt? Had he set him up to fail?

He entered the pool room in a huff and climbed the ladder to the high diving platform. Then he performed a swan dive into the gymnasium pool. His back was arched and his arms outstretched. He felt like he was sailing with the wind at his back, into the pool. The cold water surrounded him as it buoyed him to the surface. He took a gulp of air and swam under water for a length of the pool. Then he swam ten laps of the breaststroke and twenty of the crawl. Finally, he settled into a "dead man's float" on the surface of the water, allowing the tension to ease out of his entire body.

Swimming was his favorite sport. His spirits were lifting. The coach was right, he thought. I will practice and attempt the test for the black belt at the next lesson. This time I will pass.

He climbed out of the pool, showered, wrapped a purple turban around his head, dressed in a silk shirt, slacks, and his well-worn running shoes, and entered the Royal Palace. He intended to complete his latest art project, a series of dragon paintings in apricot and magenta watercolors. But when he came into the Palace he sensed all the warnings of a major crisis.

Diamante, Pachuco's three-year-old black Labrador retriever, appeared restless and out of sorts, but he thumped his tail at the sight of the King. The dog had keen intuition and sensed immediately if something were amiss among members of the royal household. Pachuco knew from the animal's agitated state that there must be a serious problem.

Queen Rosa was entering the dining room from the south portico as he entered from the north. His mother's white hair was tousled, and he noted that she was clutching her hands under her flowing burgundy robes. There were deep furrows in her brow.

"What is it?" he asked her. He ordered Diamante, who kept trying to jump on him, to keep still.

The Queen whispered to him out of the servants' earshot.

"There was a sighting last night of Malvado, the troll that destroyed your great-grandfather's Kingdom," she said. "Your father was always certain that Malvado had been killed years ago in a border skirmish. But we have in this morning's intelligence from a very reputable source that he is back and vows to devastate your Kingdom as well."

She continued to speak in hushed tones, "I am going to make this very clear. You are not to travel anywhere in the Kingdom beyond this Royal Palace's moat without your guards. I am going to add two more to your security detail. Malvado or his spies will be watching your every movement. We can't be too careful."

"But Mother," said King Pachuco, "I won't be able to visit my friends. I won't be able to take Diamante on walks outside the Palace walls to see the evening rainbows!"

"You will have to stay close to the Palace for a while," admitted the Queen. "I vow that the death or disappearance of a King must never happen in Pacifista again."

"You're right," said Pachuco soberly, wondering if the Royal Palace would become his prison. That notion sent a shiver down his spine.

Pacifista's laws of succession had made him King despite his youth when his father had perished the previous fall in a hunting accident. He could no longer lead the carefree life of a young boy. He was a sovereign and exerted a considerable influence in ruling his homeland.

The servants laid the luncheon of sliced beef, cheeses, and salads on the table in gold and crystal serving platters, but Pachuco and his mother sat motionless, as if unaware of the feast before them.

"There is something that we never told you about Malvado," said the Queen to Pachuco. "You were too young, and then we thought the danger no longer existed."

"What is that?" asked Pachuco, dreading to hear what came next.

"Your father and I always suspected," the Queen said, "that the troll had a spell that would preserve his body and allow him to be brought back to life in the near or far distant future. We hoped he had died, but somehow we never believed he was gone."

"What kind of spell?" asked Pachuco.

"It is a spell to reawaken his physical and mental powers so he can make another attempt to destroy our Kingdom."

"Do you really think he'll do this?" asked Pachuco breathlessly.

"I'm afraid that we have received convincing evidence that he has returned to bring down your Kingdom," said the Queen as she held her head in her hands.

The two picked at their lunch. "The guests for the Royal Ball will be here in a matter of hours, Pachuco," said the Queen. "Should we consider canceling the Ball?"

"Of course not," said Pachuco. "The Ball will be a success, as always. Our guards will be extra-vigilant. We have nothing to fear." He wondered if he believed this statement even as he said it.

The Queen quickly finished her lunch and took off for the Palace kitchens. It was a fine spring afternoon and Pachuco had planned to spend it exploring a trail in the woods just outside the Palace moat. He knew his mother had insisted he stay within the Palace walls, but what could happen to him on a magnificent afternoon in the sunshine with Diamante at his side?

He had been planning this hike for weeks. He had heard the scenery was spectacular on this hiking path, and this was the only afternoon when he did not have his full academic schedule of classes with his Palace tutors. He knew he should listen to his mother's warning about the sighting of the troll, but in the daylight, what could possibly happen? He had been instructed that trolls possessed their full destructive powers only from sundown to sunup.

He called Diamante who came at a gallop, and they took off for the woods.

The path they took led them to higher elevations and alpine meadows full of blooming poppies. Diamante rolled joyfully in the deep red flowers. Pachuco basked in their beauty.

Further along the trail Pachuco discovered an immense waterfall. It seemed to descend out of sheer rock cliff and cover at least 200 yards in width. Pacifista's waterfalls were not colorless like the ones on Earth. Instead, each strand of cascading water was a distinct color. The colors did not shift as if in a kaleidoscope like the colors of Pacifista's rainbows. Instead they maintained their hue until the streams of water rushed downward to become part of an azure lake hundreds of yards below. The effect was both magnificent and calming.

The tranquility of the waterfall was not lost on Pachuco who had had a most jarring morning. He sat down by the rushing water under the shade of an elm tree. Diamante stopped his rambling and settled down by Pachuco, putting his head in his lap. Before he knew it, Pachuco was lulled to sleep by the roar of the waterfall and the warmth of the sunshine.

> The wind riffling through the lush elm foliage returned Pachuco to the cold cloud of swirling, yellow leaves that marred the final hunting trip Pachuco had taken with his father. They had been hunting for deer with crossbows when a doe escaped into the dense brush with a

deafening crash. Pachuco positioned the faun trailing her in the sites of his crossbow.

"I've got him!" exclaimed Pachuco.

King Guillermo stepped in and leaned firmly on Pachuco's shooting arm with his hand.

"Let him go, Pachuco," he said. "The little one needs to run off and find his mother. We don't prey on defenseless creatures."

The golden leaves continued churning in the wind. The sight of the tossing leaves and the eerie sound of the wind set Pachuco's spine tingling and made him queasy.

"Malvado the troll can appear as a gnome, and he can change at will into a massive one-eyed giant," said the King.

"How will I recognize him if I see him?" asked Pachuco.

"He has a spider tattoo on the outside of his right hand," said King Guillermo as he tamped down the tobacco in his favorite pipe.

"If the troll should ever return in your lifetime, carry mistletoe," said King Guillermo. "Only this plant can protect you from the troll."

The tones of his father's resonating voice were somber as he said, "This troll is a demon, a threat to the domain of Pacifista. He is a force of evil."

Then his father plunged into a massive crevasse masked by the swirling carpet of leaves. His scream was haunting; he uttered no further words.

Pachuco awoke with a start, throwing Diamante off his lap. The dream had been so real, as if his father had returned to warn him about Malvado's threat and relive his final moments. Pachuco was bathed in sweat, and he was chilled though the temperature remained warm.

The sun was low on the horizon. It was essential he and Diamante return to the Palace before nightfall. Malvado would be lurking after sunset. His mother's warnings echoed in his head.

Then Pachuco remembered the Palace Ball. "Diamante, we had better race back to the Royal Palace," Pachuco sang out, nudging the sluggish Labrador retriever forward.

Pachuco decided to gather some branches of mistletoe on the way back to the castle. He remembered a thicket of the plant not too far from the trail and headed there. He located the bush and used his pocketknife to sever a few branches, which he slid into the pockets of his trousers.

Then the two ran all the way back to the Royal Palace. Both were panting by the time they reached it.

The Queen was making her way toward her throne in the ballroom when Pachuco and Diamante entered the room. A diamond tiara glittered in her carefully coifed white hair. She wore a low-cut, long black dress, its neckline studded with rubies and diamonds. Over the dress she wore a mink cloak that had been dyed a rich burgundy tone. It had a twenty-foot train that three servants carefully maneuvered as she glided gracefully across the ballroom's threshold and sat regally on her throne.

King Pachuco was relieved at the sight of his mother looking so elegant when hours before she had been on the verge of collapse. He ran to her.

"Mother, you look so pretty!" he exclaimed, hugging her briefly.

"And where have you been all afternoon? I was searching for you everywhere to help me greet the heads of State who are staying at the Royal Palace, but I managed without you. Go and dress now. The guests will arrive in half an hour."

"And don't forget to take off those sneakers," she added as an afterthought.

"Mother, will you ever stop complaining about my running shoes? They may be dirty and battered, but they are the most comfortable shoes I own. Why can't you understand that?" Pachuco scowled.

The Queen stood, gesturing to the servants to maneuver her massive cape, and walked towards the anteroom where she and Pachuco would wait to be received by the Palace royalty.

Pachuco went to his room to shower and dress. He looked over his extensive wardrobe and selected an emerald green brocade suit and black shirt with a cummerbund. On his head he wound a silk turban that was lavender with red highlights. Lastly, he begrudgingly put aside his running shoes in exchange for formal black leather footwear. The black leather shoes pinched his toes as soon as he tied them.

As he headed for the ballroom, he thought that the palace shoemaker would have to be replaced.

He forgot the mistletoe peeking out of the pockets of the trousers he left in a pile on the bedroom floor.

Diamante, who slept in his bedroom on a large pillow, had followed him when he went to his room to shower and dress. The broad, muscular dog had tried to slip out the door after him.

"No, boy," Pachuco had scolded him as he grabbed him by the scruff of the neck. "The Ball is not for you. I'll see you later tonight after the guests leave, and we'll go for a short walk."

Diamante had put his head between his paws as he settled down on his pillow. His chestnut eyes had an air of dejection, but he had remained silent. He was used to waiting for the King.

CHAPTER THREE

The Palace Ball

Mirasol lifted her skirts several inches as she climbed into the wagon as she and Fargo made their way to the Royal Palace for the Palace Ball. Fargo held a torch to light the narrow road in the darkness.

Once they had traveled about one-fourth of the distance, Fargo said, "You have become a young lady, Mirasol. You are the picture of your mother when she was your age."

Mirasol beamed. "Do you remember my parents? What were they like?" she asked.

"They were a handsome couple," recalled Fargo. "Your father was six feet tall with light hair, and your mother was petite with dark curls like yours. They both loved to hike, and your father was always studying nature and writing about it. He had several of his volumes on nature published by the Pacifista Press."

Mirasol was thrilled. Finally she had confirmation that her father, and her mother, too, had loved the natural world. Her father had even published books about nature! These must be the volumes she had discovered in the castle library. She knew her love of nature was the legacy they had left her.

Hearing about her parents delighted her, and she couldn't help but ask Fargo, who was almost like family to her, "Why doesn't Grandmother ever talk about my parents?"

Fargo hesitated. "It's not my place to say. You should rightfully hear this from your grandmother."

"You know my grandmother won't talk about my parents, Fargo," said Mirasol. "You will have to tell me what happened. I'm old enough to know."

"Well," began Fargo, hesitantly, "your parents caught an illness while camping in the swamplands where your father was studying wildlife. Your grandmother was known far and wide as a healer. She tried everything, but she could do nothing to prevent their deaths."

Mirasol was flushed and her heart quickened. "I wouldn't have been able to bear the loss of my parents if I'd been old enough to understand."

"Yes," agreed the maintenance man. "It was hard for your grandmother to carry on as well. But then she had you to take care of, and we had the castle to keep up. Finally she was able to put the mourning behind her in her own way."

By the time he had said these words, they had reached the Royal Palace. Dozens of torches lit up the outer face of the immense structure. Horses and carriages were crossing the moat and stopping at the doorway. Large numbers of elegantly dressed royalty moved into the Palace.

Fargo took Mirasol by the arm. Once over the threshold, she looked up into the gleaming chandelier with rows upon rows of tiny lighted candles. There were torches at every expanse of the grand ballroom illuminating the waxed wooden floor and the bright silver serving dishes where servants stood ready to serve appetizers and tall flutes of sparkling wine.

Mirasol could not even begin to take in the setting in which she found herself. Fargo waved farewell and disappeared down a hallway. She knew that if anyone asked her a question she would be able to do no more than stutter. She hoped that no one would approach her.

After a few minutes her heart stopped throbbing. She glanced around her and saw girls about her age lining up to be introduced to the Queen and her son who had not yet appeared.

Suddenly four groups of musicians entered and began tuning their instruments. Amidst the cacophony of sound, a palace official announced that the King and Queen would be appearing momentarily and bid them all to be silent.

The musical groups broke into a melodious tune, the likes of which Mirasol had never heard. There were all varieties of horns, from clarinets to cornets, and all seemed to brightly welcome the King and Queen with music that sounded like an echo of the mighty rushing of all of Pacifista's many waterfalls. Then in they came, the Queen with her burgundy mink cape, and the King, a tall, slender boy, at her side.

There was a moment of respectful silence and then the assembled royalty broke into fierce applause and cries of "Hail to the King and Queen." The monarchs acknowledged the appreciation of the gathering and moved to their thrones on a raised dais at one end of the large ballroom. Once settled there, those assembled presented themselves singly or in pairs as a palace official sang out their names.

Mirasol stood in line between several young girls and waited her turn to be received by the King and Queen. It took her fifteen minutes to reach the head of the line, and by then her palms and brow were damp. As it was nearing her turn, she felt faint, and was glad that her grandmother had made her practice curtsying so many times that it came naturally.

After her name was called, she presented herself to the King and Queen and curtsied deeply. The Queen graciously extended a hand to her and said, "Welcome, my dear. I don't recall seeing you at our Palace functions."

"This is my first Palace Ball," said Mirasol, as she curtsied again.

King Pachuco, who looked like he had been hit by a bolt of lightning, smiled broadly at her. He asked, "Could I please sign your dance card?"

Mirasol was so flustered that it took her several minutes to retrieve the dance card from her beaded bag. Finally she found it and gave it to the King who signed his name. He requested four dances with her.

"Thank you," she said as she nodded and moved off into the crowd. I never expected in my wildest dreams to be dancing with the King at the Royal Ball, she thought. What will Grandmother say when I tell her in the morning that I danced with the King?

A queue of young men formed around Mirasol.

"Excuse me, could I,… um…, please sign your dance card?" a young Prince stammered. He had dark hair and eyes and could barely meet her gaze.

"Why certainly," said Mirasol. She tried to put him at ease as she produced her dance card from her purse and gave it the young man to sign.

He signed it and hurried off with a satisfied smile.

Another Prince approached her and said, "Your dance card, if you will."

Mirasol did not like his tone, but her grandmother had never told her she could refuse to dance with the Palace royalty, so she produced the card and let him sign it.

Finally every space on her dance card was filled, and one of the orchestral groups struck up a stately minuet. The King led the Queen onto the dance floor as the dancing began. Mirasol observed the two and noted that the King was stiff as he whirled his mother around the dance floor. Why, it almost looks as if his shoes are too tight, she thought to herself. Imagine, a King with shoes that don't fit properly! She smiled to herself and bit her lip so she wouldn't laugh out loud. She kept thinking of her grandmother's warnings about behavior in polite society. She was sure that outright laughing would be more unwelcome than constant chatter.

Her first dancing partner found her and whisked her off to dance the stately minuet. He was a good-looking young Prince about her age and seemed to be an excellent dancer, but when they reached the end of the dance, he stepped on her instep in what seemed to be a purposeful and insulting manner.

She was in such pain that she could not help crying out.

"What's your problem?" the Prince asked. "I've done nothing. You have merely twisted your ankle."

She looked down at her dance card to find that her second partner was none other than King Pachuco.

"You stepped on her foot," said King Pachuco sternly. "I saw it with my own eyes. Apologize now!"

"I'm truly sorry," said the Prince as he flushed scarlet. "It will never happen again."

"Are you injured?" the King asked Mirasol when the Prince had departed. "Are you up for another dance?"

"Of course," said Mirasol. "Dancing is like breathing to me."

The second dance was a folk dance that Mirasol had been dancing since she was a child. She was ready for the music's fast pace. The King, however, was not as familiar with the dance and seemed hesitant as she moved easily into its complex rhythm.

He is decidedly not a skilled dancer, thought Mirasol. It's just my luck that I have to dance four dances with him! He does not look like he's enjoying dancing with me. I wonder if it's me, dancing in general, or dancing in his ill-fitting shoes that is causing his frustration.

She knew that she should be elated to be dancing so many dances with Pachuco, King of Pacifista. The truth of it was that he acted just like any other boy her age, and his lack of dancing experience was maddening. She wanted to fly on the dance floor to the fabulous music, and he couldn't keep up.

Once the dance was over, she moved on to her next partner, another young man who was an excellent dancer. They danced a tune with a syncopated beat similar to a tango. Mirasol was so engrossed in this dance that she was breathless upon its conclusion. She thanked her dancing partner and glanced at her dance card.

Another dance with King Pachuco. When Mirasol heard the first few strains of the music she knew that it was a polka set at a wildly rapid beat. She sensed that the King would not be able to keep up with her if she began this dance. She could have asked him if he wanted to sit this one out, but instead she launched into the dance with him. He lasted halfway through, and then moved off the floor.

"Is it OK if we have a drink, Mirasol?" asked Pachuco.

"Of course," she answered. He led Mirasol to a table laden with beverages of all varieties. She selected a sparkling water, and he chose a lemon juice.

"Do you like dogs?" Pachuco asked Mirasol between sips of his juice.

"Dogs?" asked Mirasol. Where had this question come from? she wondered.

"Diamante, my black Labrador retriever, is my pet. He lives at the Palace, and I take him on hikes to see the rainbows every day," he explained.

"Yes, I like dogs and all natural creatures," Mirasol responded. "But I live with my grandmother, and she won't let me have a dog."

"Where is your castle?" asked Pachuco.

"Just beyond the hill south of the Royal Palace," said Mirasol. "It's not far."

"Would you allow me to escort you back to your castle after the ball?" asked Pachuco.

Mirasol had promised her grandmother that Fargo would accompany her to the castle, but she had no qualms about accepting the invitation from the King. What could happen to her when in the company of the King, she wondered. Surely he was familiar with the vicinity near the Royal Palace, and probably he had guards that followed him everywhere. Her grandmother could not object if the King himself walked her home, could she? Besides, she would send word to Fargo that she was getting an escort home from the King and his entourage.

"Yes," answered Mirasol. "That would be fine."

The rest of the Ball passed quickly. Mirasol enjoyed the dancing immensely and only wished she had more skilled partners to dance with. The last dance was a marvelous waltz. The music was so romantic that she swooned when it was over. Her partner caught her, holding her at the waist in an intimate embrace.

Her partner was a dashing figure in a luminous blue suit. "Are you sure you are feeling well?" he asked.

"Why, yes," answered Mirasol, slightly short of breath, "I guess I got carried away by the music. I'm fine."

What would her grandmother think if she knew about this dance, Mirasol thought. She looked around and wondered if anyone had observed her who might get word back to Lupita. She could just see her grandmother with one eyebrow raised and her hands on her hips.

"Haven't I raised you better than this?" she would shout. "As soon as my back is turned you embrace a member of the Royal Court on the dance floor at your first Palace Ball! What happened to your Court etiquette?"

Mirasol also wondered what Pachuco would think if he saw her nearly fainting into the arms of a Prince at the close of a waltz. She tossed her curly head. He had no right to criticize her just because he had offered to escort her home. She felt like stamping her foot. Why she barely knew him, and he couldn't even dance!

As the dancing concluded, the assembled royalty moved into the room adjoining the ballroom that had been set with rows of round tables. Each table was covered with a linen tablecloth, eight ornate place settings, and a centerpiece of pale lavender orchids. Across one wall was a large rectangular table where the King and Queen and other notable royalty would sit.

Mirasol took a seat as far from the royal table as she could get. Two girls her age soon joined her.

"Did you see the King?" one of them gushed. "Isn't he handsome?"

Mirasol was silent. She hadn't considered whether he were handsome or not. The two looked at her expectantly.

"I guess so," she answered finally.

"He's a dream," said the second young girl as she pushed her hair away from her face. "I sure would like to have had his name on my dance card."

Mirasol held her tongue. She certainly was not going to reveal that he was one of the worst dancers in the room. Her grandmother would have been proud of her self-control.

Before long a line of servants brought course after course of the late night feast. There were quail, squid, lobster and roasted meats of all varieties. Mirasol tasted a few of the less exotic dishes. She found them gamy for the most part and had to hide a few bites balled up in her napkin. Her grandmother had warned her not to eat too much lest some of the royalty think she was not properly fed at home.

Then she sat and waited while those around her finished their dinners and drank wine. Dessert was flaming custard, which she found far too sweet for her taste.

Those sitting at the head table made numerous toasts to the King and Queen who returned the favor.

Finally the Ball was drawing to a close. Those in attendance gathered up their belongings and started in the direction of the mammoth front doors of the Royal Palace. Mirasol was thinking that Fargo might come for her before King Pachuco did, but she was wrong.

King Pachuco appeared out of the crowd, took her hand in his, and rushed her out of the dining room.

"We are going to leave by a side door that few people in the Royal Palace know," said Pachuco.

"Why is that?" asked Mirasol.

"Just to avoid all the people going to their carriages," answered Pachuco. He told the head of his security entourage to follow ten paces behind as he escorted Mirasol to her castle.

Mirasol sent a message to Fargo telling him that the King and his security guards were escorting her home.

They exited the side door and found themselves in the cool air. The night was dark as the moon and stars were hidden behind thick clouds. The two set off for Mirasol's castle at a rapid clip.

CHAPTER FOUR

The Troll

Pachuco and Mirasol walked quickly through the fog. It became increasingly difficult to see more than ten paces ahead, and their steps slowed. The young King began to regret having instructed his security detail to follow ten paces behind. He could barely discern the forms of the soldiers trailing them in military formation.

Three-quarters of the way to Mirasol's castle, there was a fork in the road marked by a great pine tree that a constant wind had caused to lean close to the ground. It was here that the breeze became blustery. Pachuco's heart was throbbing; he felt weak.

The fierce wind, dense fog, and his mother's stern warnings came together to inspire fear in the young King.

"Are you feeling well?" asked Mirasol. "You look flushed, even feverish."

"I'm fine," answered Pachuco. Take my hand, Mirasol," he demanded. "Just in case . . . ."

"In case what?" Mirasol wanted to know. "What's going on?"

"I can't explain it all right now," said Pachuco, though he believed that he owed her some explanation, especially if danger were at hand. "There's a troll who killed my great-grandfather who may have returned to threaten my Kingdom."

"How could he do that unless he was over a hundred years old?" asked Mirasol, who was obviously good at mental arithmetic.

"He has magical powers…." began Pachuco.

Just then a huge branch of the pine tree fell with a roar in front of the pair. Mirasol let out a high-pitched scream, and Pachuco, who was standing closer to the branch, moved away and pulled Mirasol with him to avoid its impact.

When both recovered their composure, they saw a troll standing atop the massive tree branch as if claiming his territory. He was only as tall as a six-year-old child but had wizened features that made him look centuries old. His feet were unusually large and fleshy and barely fit into his leather shoes that had holes in them through which his toes seemed to ooze. He had a long white beard and wore a red cap and a craftsman's leather apron. His body gave off the sharp odor of mildewed socks that made Pachuco queasy.

Was this troll a kind forest-dweller, or was he Malvado, evil personified?

King Pachuco stared at the top of the troll's right hand. Where was the identifying mark? he wondered. The dwarf was so small and moved so swiftly that it took him thirty seconds to locate the spider tattoo. Beads of perspiration popped out on Pachuco's forehead. Then he spotted it. The tattoo was faint but it was clearly the mark of a spider. *Yes, it was Malvado!*

"We are just returning from the Palace Ball," said Mirasol to the troll. "We are on the way to my castle. How nice to make your acquaintance."

Pachuco noted that Mirasol was back to using her Court etiquette tone. The problem with that was she would have to engage Malvado in conversation until dawn for them to have a chance of escaping his destructive powers. Otherwise polite conversation with the troll would probably be of no consequence.

The King remembered that on his walk that afternoon with Diamante he had cut some mistletoe branches and put them in his trouser pockets. Now he fished around in his pockets hoping to find the branches. No luck. The wrong pants, he thought with crushing dismay. The branches are in my other pants!

The troll remained perched on the thick branch and made no move to let the pair pass.

"Malvado, let us proceed," Pachuco pleaded. "We have done nothing to you. You have no reason to stop us."

"I most certainly do," said Malvado whose high-pitched voice came out in a squeaky whimper. "Pacifista has been ruled by trolls for centuries before your family came to power, and we will conquer it again. You are but a boy. And a poor excuse for a King."

Pachuco flushed at this remark, but he took several deep breaths and tried to remain calm. He remembered the advice of his martial arts coach that energy should not be wasted on emotion in times of great stress.

"We will see who the true monarch of Pacifista is," said Pachuco. "Let me take my friend home, and then we will settle the score."

"No, you are not going to get away that easily," said Malvado. "Your great-grandfather scoffed at my powers. That is why I destroyed him, and that is why I am going to destroy you."

"No," Mirasol called out when she heard the troll's threat.

"Please, leave Mirasol out of this. She is a Princess, and not an especially high-placed one at that. She needs to return to her castle tonight," said the King.

"I will decide what happens tonight. This young girl is a member of the Royal Court, and she's with you. Her fate is sealed with yours," said Malvado. "You no longer have any authority in Pacifista. Mark my words. Both of you cannot escape my powers."

"And by the way," continued the troll, "don't look for assistance from your vast security detail. They are all lying unconscious in the road. They will not awaken, if at all, until twenty-four hours have elapsed."

The boy knew that with his knowledge of the martial arts he could take on the troll physically and win. But he could not have imagined Malvado's next move.

All at once the troll let out a fierce roar. His child-like stature was replaced with one of a giant hairy beast, over ten feet tall. His eyes bulged hideously, his fur was a foot long, and his huge belly dragged on the floor of the woods.

Out of the corner of his eye, Pachuco could see Mirasol's face turning as white as her ball gown. Her whole body seemed to be quaking.

Pachuco took an inventory of all the martial arts moves he knew and decided he might be able to use Malvado's own momentum to throw him to the ground. The creature was immense, but there was a chance that he could take him.

Pachuco ordered Mirasol to move to the side of the road.

"No, I'm not budging," protested Mirasol. "I can help you in this fight."

"Move out of the way!" said Pachuco. "This is not going to be pretty."

Mirasol stepped aside, and Pachuco charged Malvado who came running at him. The setup was fine, but when he tried to latch onto the troll's arm, it seemed to be locked in place, and Pachuco could barely execute a roll to avoid serious injury.

"You are making a mistake," said Mirasol to Pachuco. "You are provoking the beast. If you use force, he will never let us go."

"Well, what do you suggest, Mirasol?" asked Pachuco.

"Let's find out what he wants," said the girl. "Maybe we can bargain with him."

"That's ridiculous," said Pachuco. "How can you bargain with a force of pure evil?"

Mirasol took a few steps closer to the troll and with a melodious voice asked him what they could give him. "Would you like a fiefdom, a chancellorship, a place in the Royal Palace? We can easily arrange any or all of these," she assured the beast diplomatically.

Pachuco cringed, imagining the Queen's reaction to these suggestions.

"I will be King," Malvado roared. "Nothing else will do, little girl. You can talk to me for hours; nothing will change my mind."

Mirasol managed to take Pachuco aside. "Why not promise Malvado that he will be King?" she asked.

"Not on your life—or mine," said Pachuco firmly.

Pachuco and Mirasol were running out of options. Pachuco decided that they should make a run for it. The troll was blocking the road leading to Mirasol's palace, and the bodies of the Palace guards were strewn across the road back to the Royal Palace. Pachuco knew if they could run in the opposite direction from the troll until the morning light, they would be home free. He and Mirasol were young and fit and certainly could outrun the ten-foot tall giant with the huge belly. Pachuco approached Mirasol and whispered to her that they should take off into the forest that surrounded the road on all sides. "It's our only chance," he said. "Do you think you can run in those boots?"

"Yes," she nodded.

"OK, on the count of five, we'll take off through the woods on the east side of the road," directed the King. "One, two, three, four, five!"

They dashed off through the woods in the fog and darkness. They ran over roots and brambles, but nothing stopped them. On and on they ran, chests heaving, seemingly unaware that they were out of breath. Finally they stopped beside a stream to drink and rest for a moment before they continued on.

"Are you all right, Mirasol?" asked Pachuco.

"Why yes, I'm fine," she answered. "The only problem is that my gown is getting muddy and torn. My grandmother and I worked on this ball gown for a year. She will be beside herself."

They ran further and further into the inky woods. They sensed the presence of the troll trailing them because rabbits, chipmunks, and night owls were running in fright. Though they could not see Malvado, they could smell his overpowering odor invading the forest.

They also had no notion of where they were, but Pachuco knew that directions would become clear to him in the daylight. If they just kept moving until dawn, they would be safe.

"It will only be a few hours, Mirasol," said the King. "We just have to keep on the move until daybreak."

Mirasol nodded. Branches had cut her face and beads of blood appeared. One sleeve of her dress was hanging by threads. Her white shoes with the buttons up the side were muddy. The jasmine garland that had graced her black curls was gone. Her silk gloves had jagged holes in them.

"We'll make it," Mirasol told Pachuco, apparently trying to buoy his spirits.

Pachuco also looked the worse for wear. He had lost his lavender turban with its red highlights. His emerald green suit jacket and black cummerbund were nowhere to be seen. He wore only his black silk shirt and slacks. His hair was tangled and hung down his back. He had discarded his black leather footwear and socks and was running barefoot. He was used to hiking without shoes if his running shoes were not handy. Still, he wished that he were wearing those running shoes!

They took off again into the forest. Animals foraging or hunting in the night scurried into the brush when they sensed the pair's footsteps. They glimpsed raccoons, squirrels, and deer running from their swift approach.

The two ran on and on through the fog. Adrenaline pumping, Pachuco never seemed to tire. "Maybe I should take up running when this is over," said Pachuco. "I'm beginning to enjoy it."

"Speak for yourself," said Mirasol, whose increasingly bedraggled ball gown was impeding her movement more and more. "I am exhausted. I don't know if I can move another step, Pachuco. Maybe you should go on without me."

"Never, Mirasol. Dawn is only a half hour away," he said, trying to encourage her to move forward. "We must get through this together."

Just then a giant elm tree in their path burst into flame. They both screamed as the burning timbers fell in their path.

The two narrowly missed running into the fiery branches. When the smoke cleared, they saw none other than the troll, in his elfin form, staring accusatorily at them.

"So you thought you could run away from me, did you?" he asked, shaking a narrow forefinger with a three-inch fingernail in their faces. "There is no way to escape. I told you this."

Pachuco, also bedraggled and exhausted, would not admit defeat, even to himself. Mirasol was biting her lip and seemed terrified.

"We will never give in to you without a fight," Pachuco said. "Pacifista is my Kingdom and my home, and I will defend it to the death."

"Then that's what it shall be," said Malvado. "You and your great-grandfather made the same choices."

"No," shrieked Mirasol. "There must be some other way. We are too young to die."

"How unfortunate," said the troll, scratching the white beard that reached a point six inches below his chin. "Strange that you would think of this now after leading me on a merry chase through the forest half the night. I have no mercy to show you as you have listened to nothing that I've said."

Pachuco gave Mirasol a knowing glance. He regretted his offer to escort her to her castle. This was a situation that involved his rule and his Kingdom. And now they were both facing grave danger.

"All right," said Pachuco to Malvado. "What are your requirements for the fight? We must choose our weapons."

"We will fight with our fists," said the troll.

"But you have black magic," noted Pachuco.

"And you have knowledge of the martial arts," said Malvado. "I would say it's an even match."

"I'd say it is not an even match at all," said Pachuco.

"It doesn't matter in the least if you object to my terms," said Malvado. "I am in control here."

"Give me twenty minutes to prepare and we will get this competition under way," said Pachuco.

"No," said the troll, sensing that dawn was minutes away.

Pachuco whispered to Mirasol that she should take off for her castle as soon as the battle began. "Don't worry about me," he said. "Go home while the troll is occupied, and you can escape."

He did not want Mirasol to leave him alone to battle the troll, but, above all, he wanted her to be safe.

Pachuco focused on his opponent, concentrated, and controlled his breathing. Everything his martial arts coach had been teaching him for years was coming naturally to him. He felt centered and poised for action.

Malvado moved towards Pachuco. In his left hand was a wand he had been hiding in one of the pockets in his apron. He waved it high in the air.

Pachuco stepped forward and knocked the wand out of Malvado's hand. The troll crawled on the ground, defenseless for a moment. Pachuco lunged for the wand. The troll soon righted himself and grabbed the wand from Pachuco's grasp.

Meanwhile Mirasol, ever on the ready, picked up a massive rock from the roadside and hurled it with all of her strength toward the troll's head. It almost hit its mark, but Malvado ducked at the last moment and managed to dodge the projectile.

Pachuco attacked with a classic martial arts move that he had been practicing for years, but the troll anticipated the attack and rolled nimbly out of danger. Pachuco was panting by this time, but he launched a well-planted kick that the troll managed to sidestep. The troll may have been small but he was amazingly quick. He displayed an uncanny ability to anticipate Pachuco's every move, no matter how well executed.

Finally Pachuco swiveled and assaulted the troll with all his force. He was flushed and feverish with concentration. This was not a sparring match with his martial arts coach. It was the ultimate struggle to determine the fate of the Kingdom of Pacifista.

Malvado grinned and effortlessly pinned Pachuco to the ground.

"I am the victor," roared the troll. "And don't you ever forget it!"

He took his wand and held it over Pachuco's head. Then he did the same to Mirasol.

"You two will never return to Pacifista as King and Princess," pronounced Malvado.

Blackness descended over Pachuco and Mirasol just as the fog lifted and dawn broke in tones of peach and lilac over the Kingdom of Pacifista.

CHAPTER FIVE

Pachuco Transformed

When the blackness descended, Pachuco was floating, lighter than air, on a weightless journey through space and time. He had lost track of the troll, Mirasol, and the Kingdom of Pacifista. He was alone on this voyage, and he wondered where it would take him. Would he ever see his loved ones again and be restored to his throne? Was this death, the final journey? These questions flashed across his mind, causing him to be bathed in perspiration, but his exhaustion won over his fear, and he soon drifted into a deep, dreamless sleep.

When he became conscious again many hours later, he was still immersed in darkness. The floating sensation was gone, and he was no longer moving. He heard sounds around him like the cheeping of birds. Curious and eager to orient himself to his new surroundings, he tried but was unable to open his eyes.

Suddenly he was gasping for breath. He became aware that his body was curled within a spherical object that fit his shape perfectly. Instinctively, he moved towards the flat end of the sphere and breathed oxygen stored there into his lungs. Acting on impulse, he set about the process of destroying his prison. His very survival meant breaking out. He had no idea what lay beyond the boundaries of the sphere, but he knew escape was necessary.

He used a strange, sharp bulge he discovered on his head to create a hole in the air sac at the flat end of the oval. He used all the energy he could muster to shatter the sphere that surrounded him. After almost an hour, cracks formed in the globe and pieces of it fell away. A welcome light source warmed his wet body.

He emerged from the oval in stages. First his head appeared. Then his upper body, and finally his lower body surfaced. He was immersed in sticky goo, and after all this effort he was still unable to open his eyes.

Fatigue struck again. He could not lift his neck or his head. He tried, but standing upright was impossible. He could only bask in the heat of the light source and listen to the loud twittering of birds that seemed to be inches away from him.

After what seemed like hours, he was able to pry open one eye and focus on the scene around him. He was surrounded by eight parrot chicks! All were chirping raucously. They were housed in a wooden box and were wallowing in the warmth of the electric light. When they opened their mouths to peep, their caretaker emptied the contents of a long syringe into their beaks, one by one.

"What am I doing here?" roared Pachuco. "I am the King of Pacifista."

But when he opened his mouth to speak, nothing came out but a shrill squeak. Again he bellowed, "I am the King. I am not a bird!"

The store owner, apparently believing Pachuco to be hungry, shot a syringe full of liquid food into his mouth.

Pachuco choked, protesting loudly.

Finally he downed the food and studied his companions. Some of the parrot chicks had wet and matted feathers like his; others that had hatched first were drying off. Fluffy fuzz was replacing their drenched feathers.

For the first time Pachuco allowed himself to look down at his body. He observed a slightly rounded midsection attached to two skinny legs that ended in talons.

"Malvado has transformed me into a parrot!" he shouted.

Pachuco's eyes glowered. His cheeks were flushed and his stomach lurched. The formula he had swallowed had tasted like sour milk, and he thought he was going to be sick. He began to take it all in: he was cut off from his home in Pacifista, his throne, his mother, Diamante, and even Princess Mirasol, the spirited young girl whom he had just met but liked very much. And he was not even in a human form. He could no longer deny the fact that Malvado had transformed him into a parrot chick.

At that moment, a bell attached to the front door of the shop rang and a young woman entered. She wore blue jeans, a tank top, and a pair of chartreuse sneakers on her narrow feet. Pachuco found her appearance pleasing. He thought back to the well-worn sneakers he had left on his bedroom floor in Pacifista.

"I heard the Lilac-headed Amazons were hatching today," she said, addressing the shopkeeper.

"Yes," he said. "They are out of their shells, and they all look healthy enough. I'm giving them their first feeding now."

"They sure took a beating from their birthing," said the woman, observing the limp hatchlings. "Where did these birds come from?"

"Mexico or another country in Central America," said the shopkeeper. "Why don't you let me reserve one of them for you? Take your pick."

"When will they be ready for sale?" asked the woman.

"In six weeks or so," answered the store owner.

"I'll be back to see them then. Thanks," said the woman and left. The bell clanged again as she took her leave.

Pachuco wished that the woman with the green sneakers would choose him as her bird. He could imagine her feeding him delicacies and allowing him to romp freely through her home.

The woman's brief conversation with the shopkeeper offered Pachuco the first clues as to his whereabouts. He was in a country not far from Central America. He had learned from his astronomy tutor on Pacifista that the Americas were on a planet known as Earth. Earth was not in his planet's galaxy, but lay in the Milky Way, a neighboring galaxy not far from his own.

Now I'm making progress, he thought, I am beginning to pin down my location, though he had to admit that as a Lilac-headed Amazon in a wooden box, he had no idea how he would begin to plan his return to Pacifista. But he swore that he would return home, regardless of the troll's ominous predictions.

As he was dreaming of his return voyage, one of his sibling Lilac-headed Amazons sidled up to him. "My name is Oscar. What was that you said before about being a King?"

"Did you understand me?" asked Pachuco.

"Why, yes," answered Oscar. "All of us hatchlings speak the same language. Didn't you know that?"

"No," said Pachuco, "I had no idea we could communicate. I am King Pachuco of Pacifista, from a neighboring galaxy," said Pachuco. "Can you believe that I am a King who has been transformed into a parrot?"

"Yes," said Oscar, "I think the transformation from a King to a parrot is the most natural thing in the world."

From that day onward, Pachuco and Oscar were fast friends. They ate together and slept side by side in the wooden box. At the same moment, they both lost their "egg teeth," the bony bulges that they had used to break open their shells. They shed their matted birth feathers at the same time and developed shiny green plumage with accents of black, blue, and red. Above their heads, a band of red plumage appeared along with a bluish-purple streak on the top of their heads. The other birds were similar in coloring, but Pachuco and Oscar were nearly identical, and most visitors to the pet shop were unable to tell them apart. The pet shop owner was the only one who could.

Pachuco and Oscar spent all their waking hours together. Pachuco told Oscar about life in the Palace and his struggle with Malvado. Oscar made up convincing yarns about where life would take him when he left the pet shop.

"When I am old enough to be adopted," predicted Oscar, "I'll live with a family of twelve children who will carry me around on their backs and feed me tortilla chips and fresh salsa. We'll race up and down the halls of their house, and their dogs will give me rides on their backs," said Oscar.

"Will they have a black Labrador?" asked Pachuco, losing himself in Oscar's fantasy. "I have a black Lab at the Palace on Pacifista."

"Yes, they'll have a black Lab and a miniature Schnauzer," said Oscar. "But no cats. I don't think I could live with animals that have claws and creep around stealthily."

"Just dogs," agreed Pachuco. "Way to go."

Pachuco and Oscar and the other parrots soon outgrew their wooden box, and they moved to a twenty-foot tall cage surrounded by steel bars.

Pachuco had not forgotten the woman with the green sneakers and often wished that she would return and take him home with her. One day the bell on the shop door clanged, and there she was! Pachuco held his breath. She was his ticket out of this prison-like cage. She walked over to the cage and carefully observed each young Lilac-headed Amazon.

Pick me! Pick me! begged Pachuco silently, jumping up and down on the highest perch in the cage. He was barely able to keep his balance.

Finally she called the shopkeeper to her side. "I have picked this one," she said, pointing to none other than Oscar.

Pachuco squawked and flew wildly all over the cage. His heart was racing in his chest. "Take me and Oscar, too," he shrieked to the woman in the chartreuse sneakers who stared at him blankly.

"No, Oscar, you can't go! What will I do without you?" he called to his friend. "You know we cannot be separated."

But try as Pachuco did to prevent the woman with the green sneakers from buying Oscar, there was nothing he could do. The shopkeeper put Oscar in a smaller cage and gave the woman a book on parrot care. She paid the bill and marched out the door with Pachuco's best friend.

Pachuco and Oscar exchanged a final, tender glance as the door closed.

That night when the other birds were snoring in the cage, Pachuco could barely hold back his tears. My Kingdom, my mother, Diamante, Mirasol, and now Oscar, he thought. It's too much.

Pachuco slept little that night, and the next day he had no appetite. He stayed in one corner of the cage and stared at the shoppers who considered purchasing one of the eight remaining Amazons. No one was interested in him, and that was fine with him.

The shopkeeper seemed to notice Pachuco's inactivity. "You're missing your mate, aren't you?" he asked him. He gave the bird some tasty millet cakes that he did not share with the other Amazons, and said to him, "You are my special buddy. I know someone will buy you soon."

Pachuco did not touch the millet and barely grazed his other food. He dreamed about Oscar and the woman with the green sneakers. He awoke in fits and starts all through the night. He was no longer preening his feathers carefully each day, and they did not gleam as before. I bet I don't look like Oscar any more, thought Pachuco.

Then, not too many days later, Pachuco's spirits rallied. Only four other Lilac-headed Amazons remained in the cage, and they approached him and offered him their friendship. They warmly welcomed him into their circle. They chattered and preened each other the whole day long and slept together through the long nights with their talons and wings touching. Oscar had been his soul mate, but these four became friends who supported him when he needed them. Surrounded by these four Amazons, his appetite returned and he slept easily and well. He was well groomed and healthy once more.

Just when Pachuco had settled into a routine with the four remaining parrots, an old couple entered the pet shop.

"Amazon parrots!" the man exclaimed. "I have seen many of these birds in my country."

He spoke proper English with a slight Mexican accent.

"How adorable," cooed the woman, surveying the other pets in the store with interest. She looked like she would have been equally happy with a puppy or a white rabbit.

"Are you sure it's a parrot that we want?" she asked her husband.

"I won't have any other animal," he answered.

The man studied the Amazons, who were by this time ten weeks old and mature hatchlings. He seemed to know his birds, and he had his well-trained eye on Pachuco, who was embarrassed by the attention and tried to disappear behind the other parrots.

"Come out, and let the man have a look at you," said the shopkeeper. "Since when are you bashful?"

Pachuco kept hiding. These folks are old; they are nothing like the woman with the chartreuse sneakers, he thought. They are not wearing sneakers at all, but heavy leather foot coverings that he later learned were hiking boots.

I don't know anything about these people and I don't want to live with them, said Pachuco to himself. I'd rather stay with my Amazon friends in the cage with the steel bars.

But the shopkeeper had other ideas. He approached the man who appeared to have taken a liking to Pachuco.

"If you take this bird, I will give you a large cage at half price," he offered.

"Lower the price and throw in a sack of sunflower seeds at no cost," said the man. Bargaining seemed to come easy to him.

The shopkeeper paused and appeared to consider the offer. "I have become attached to these Amazons, but I know it's time for them to find homes. Give me cash and it's a deal," he said.

The old man opened his wallet and counted out the bills as Pachuco looked on with a frightened gleam flashing in his eyes. His tail feathers fanned out and his wing feathers spread. The other birds looked on warily.

The old couple picked a roomy cage, and the shopkeeper transferred Pachuco to his new home. The man slung the sack of sunflower seeds on his shoulder, hoisted the cage, and headed out of the shop. The woman followed her husband.

Pachuco squawked a farewell to the other Amazons who responded with forlorn cheeps.

"What will we call the parrot?" she asked her husband when they were settled in the car.

"Let's sleep on it," he replied. "A name will come to us in the night."

Pachuco lurched on the highest perch on the cage as the old man put the 1978 Chevy pickup into gear and took off. He looked around as his surroundings flashed past at an alarming rate. His heart skipped a beat, and he yearned for his mother, the forests of Pacifista, Mirasol, and his friend Oscar.

The next morning the couple awoke and went to the kitchen to uncover the bird.

When the old woman removed the sheet from his cage, Pachuco gazed at the couple with one discerning eye and let out a faint squawk.

"*Buenos días*," said the old man to the Amazon.

"Good morning, green boy," said the old woman.

The old couple prepared beans, rice, and tortillas with chile thrown in for his first breakfast. It was the same food they ate themselves. Pachuco found the smell of the food enticing, but he was too nervous to venture down to the food bowl in his cage to taste it. He munched on a few sunflower seeds and peanuts instead, food that he recognized from the pet store.

"Have you thought about the parrot's name?" asked the woman. "I was thinking of Jorge, or perhaps Juan."

"Jorge or Juan! Not on your life," exclaimed Pachuco.

"I have decided that his name will be *Pachuco*," said the old man. "It suits him."

"That's an unusual name," said the old woman, "How did you come up with it?"

"It came to me in a dream," said the old man.

"All right," agreed the old woman, "Pachuco it will be."

What an amazing coincidence, thought Pachuco. The man is calling me by the name I was given on Pacifista. Maybe I *was* meant to live here with the old couple.

For the first time since the Palace Ball he had a sense of well-being. He was still living behind steel bars, but his name had returned to him, the name he had been given in his planet in the next galaxy from the Milky Way. Could other miracles be in store for him on this planet they called Earth?

CHAPTER SIX

Pachuco Settles In

P achuco stood like a statue on the highest perch of his cage
for the first week in the old couple's kitchen. His head
tilted to enable one deep brown eye to take in the scene.
His eyes were completely surrounded by white feathers as if he
were wearing a thin application of eyeliner.

Pachuco was lonely without the company of the four hatchlings,
jostling and twittering in their steel cage. He was used to his
companions good-naturedly competing for the tastiest morsels of
food. He thought about Oscar, and how they had evenly divided
their food between them. He was not accustomed to eating alone
with the old couple seated nearby at the kitchen table looking on.
He felt ill at ease and had no appetite.

"Why doesn't Pachuco touch his food?" asked the old woman.

"Give him time," the old man answered. "We are his flock now. He
will eat when we do."

When the couple left the Amazon's cage open, Pachuco threw
caution to the wind and ventured out of the cage and onto the old
woman's left wrist. She brought some food up to his beak and tried

to hand feed him pinto beans, corn, and bits of tortilla. He nervously dug his talons deep into the woman's wrist, leaving a red mark. She winced in pain, but continued her effort to feed him.

Pachuco admitted to himself that the food smelled delicious, but he still could not bring himself to open his beak and taste it. He was sure it would beat seeds and millet, the fare at the pet shop. He took a good whiff of the food the old woman offered him and climbed to the top of the cage, hoisting his body with his beak.

What were Oscar and the woman with the chartreuse sneakers doing now? he wondered. If only he could live with them! He did not want to stay with the old man and old woman who were far older than even his mother, Queen Rosa. Why, they were old enough to be his grandparents, he thought. This will never do.

Suddenly he began to fly, lifting off and extending his colorful wings. He swooped low over the heads of the old man and the old woman. Flying was a new experience for him. In the pet shop he had never left his cage. In the old couple's house, he flew with abandon, a freedom he had never experienced on Pacifista. Not even while swimming, his favorite sport, had he felt this unconfined. Flying came naturally to him, though he had no idea how he was doing it. I don't even think I could explain flying to my martial arts coach on Pacifista, thought Pachuco. I could probably show him the movements, but I'm sure I couldn't explain how I perform them.

Sounds from the den interrupted Pachuco's thoughts.

"I'm making a perch for you so you can be with us while we read or watch television in the den," said the old man as he sawed a tree branch, stripped its bark, and secured it to a cardboard box with a long metal bolt.

The Amazon was unable to focus on the images in the black box that the couple called the "television," but he could hear voices and sound coming from it, some of which he found terrifying. He could not comprehend what the old couple found fascinating about this machine.

Pachuco also observed the man fashioning a swing of wood and metal for him. When he was finished, the old man placed Pachuco on the swing and gave him a firm push. Pachuco swung back and forth, tightly gripping the bottom perch with his talons. This contraption is unsettling, he thought, as the swing shifted rapidly back and forth. I can barely hang on with my talons, and it kicks up a breeze that is ruffling my feathers. When he had had enough of the harsh ride on the swing, he flew back to the top perch of his cage, a location where he was beginning to feel some sense of security.

"That's enough of the swing for today?" asked the old man. "Don't worry; we'll try it again tomorrow."

"Let the bird be," protested the old woman. "Can't you see that he's not comfortable with us? He's not eating, and he's losing weight. His feathers have lost some of the luster they had when he came to us."

"Give him time," said the old man. "That's all he needs."

Finally, after slightly more than a week, Pachuco approached his feeding dish when the couple had sat down for breakfast. Before they knew it, he had gobbled up its entire contents.

"He is eating!" exclaimed the old woman. "I'm going to give him more beans and rice. What a relief!"

Pachuco had been famished. He discovered the food the old couple prepared tasted wonderful. It was unlike any food he had ever tasted on Pacifista, but it was delicious.

After Pachuco began to eat regularly, the old man taught the Amazon to speak a mixture of Spanish and English. His first words were: *"Ese Pachuco, bato loco, baby, baby, baby boy."*

Pachuco's voice was thick and raspy and surprised him. Is that voice really coming from me? he wondered. His parrot voice seemed to have no relation to his evolving bass on Pacifista.

The old woman worked with him, too, and he added to his repertoire "I love you," and "How are you?"

One morning he greeted the old woman with the phrase, "How I love you."

She appeared bewildered. She told her husband about the incident and said, "I never taught him to say 'How I love you.' Can you believe that he is inventing phrases?"

Her husband showed no surprise. "Amazons are extremely bright birds," he said. "Never underestimate them."

In those first few weeks Pachuco began to mimic sounds he heard around him. He could make the sound of the phone ringing and send the old woman running to answer it to find no one on the other end. The old man would take the bird into the bathroom in the morning, and Pachuco could soon mimic the sound of the man using his old-fashioned hand shaver and brushing his teeth.

The Amazon parrot often thought about his life on Pacifista and wondered if Malvado's rule were destroying the Kingdom. What had happened to his mother, the Royal Palace, and Diamante, his black Labrador? Would his mother forgive him for taking off in the night after the Palace Ball? Would he manage to escape and return to the country of his birth? And if he did manage to return to Pacifista, how would anyone believe he was Pachuco the King disguised in the form of a Lilac-headed Amazon parrot? Had his vast security detail revived? And what had become of Mirasol? Would he ever see her again? He thought about these questions as he stood on the top perch in his cage, balancing easily on a single talon.

Pachuco began to enjoy the old couple when they were entertaining. They would invite friends and the old man's extended Hispanic family for a fiesta. From his kitchen vantage point, he watched the couple cooking for several days, making trays of enchiladas, a baked dish made with corn tortillas, cheese, chicken or beef, and New Mexican green chile. They also cooked huge pots of the famous New Mexican green chile stew, a thick soup containing pork simmered for hours on the stovetop with potatoes, herbs, and green chile.

The couple had a garden in their yard and grew *habañero* chile, the hottest chile on Planet Earth. Pachuco and the old man loved food cooked with this New Mexican chile, but the old woman could not eat it. She would make a mild *salsa* with homegrown *tomatillos*, a spicy green vegetable, *jalapeño* chile, and tomatoes that she served with mounds of tortilla chips. Tortilla chips dipped in this salsa were high on Pachuco's growing list of favorite foods.

Before the company arrived, Pachuco observed the couple rolling up the rugs in the living and dining rooms to prepare for dancing after dinner. There were often few male dancers, and the old man, a skilled dancer, took every woman out on the dance floor for a spin.

"Sorry, Pachuco, but you have to stay in your cage during the party. You might perch on someone's plate to have a bite or land on someone's head," said the old man, who wheeled his cage into the living room so that he could watch the dancing. The guests admired him, and he basked in the attention. The partygoers fed him at every opportunity, as did the old woman, so his food dish was overflowing with goodies.

The old man never took him to bed at 8:00 p.m. on party nights. He loved to see the partygoers dancing the bright salsa dances. He delighted in the fact that some of the most graceful dancers were the largest people. Why, that is just like me, he thought. I am a rather large bird, but I am an expert flyer. Size and grace can go hand in hand.

When Pachuco stood on a single talon and his eyes began to shut, he was almost ready for sleep. The old woman wheeled his cage back to the kitchen and covered it with his sheet. Then he climbed up to the top perch for the night. He could still hear sounds of the music and dancing drifting in from the living room.

At the end of his first month with the old couple, the two were again preparing for a party. The woman was grilling marinated chicken for twenty friends from the neighborhood. Just as she put the chicken on the grill with the fire dramatically flaring, the telephone rang.

"Pachuco, you had better not be mimicking the sound of the telephone," she called out as she ran in from the back porch.

Pachuco was dozing and opened one eye in an effort to understand what she was talking about.

The woman answered the phone and listened for a few minutes. She appeared to be speaking to an *amiga* who was coming to the party with her husband.

When the old woman had hung up the phone, the old man came into the kitchen. "It's the oddest thing," the old woman told her husband. "Our friends who live on the far side of the mountains want to know if Pachuco has a traveling cage. They say they've found a parakeet and want to bring it to us."

"What did you tell them?" asked the old man.

"I told them to bring it over, though I don't know how Pachuco will take to it. He's used to being an only child," said the old woman.

The old man nodded.

Pachuco napped as he heard the old woman continue to grill and set up for the party. When the friends from the far side of the mountains arrived an hour later, Pachuco had all but forgotten the telephone call about the parakeet. He had seen parakeets in the pet shop but had never thought twice about them. Pachuco was busy eating grilled chicken and gnawing on chicken bones. He tore into the brittle bones with his beak and ate the marrow inside them.

Despite his feasting, the sight of the shoebox that the man from the mountains carried under his arm aroused Pachuco's curiosity. What was in the shoebox? Some new style of shoes? He had observed that these inhabitants of Earth were constantly changing their shoe styles.

Pachuco noticed holes punched in the shoebox across its top and sides. How curious, thought Pachuco. Could there be something alive in the box?

The old woman took the box from her friend and announced, "I've found the small bird cage in the shed, washed it down, and added water and seeds for the parakeet."

She opened the shoebox and let out a gasp of surprise.

"Why, this is no parakeet!" she exclaimed. "This is a lovebird. It's beautiful!"

The old man stood beside her and peered over her shoulder into the box. He smiled. "You're right. A peach-throated lovebird at that. She is a classy little bird, if I've ever seen one."

Pachuco observed everyone in the kitchen crowd around the box.

"Let's get her into the cage," said the old woman. "She looks like she needs a drink." She asked her friends how long the lovebird was outside on such a hot summer afternoon.

"For an hour at least," said her *amiga*. "I heard her cheeping and called all over the neighborhood to see if anyone had lost a bird.

No one had so we climbed up on the roof, scooped her up, and put her in the shoebox. She put up quite a fight; she's a fierce little bird. We put a container with water in the box when we drove over, but I think most of it spilled in the car."

Pachuco was listening to this conversation with open ears. A peach-throated lovebird? This was something rare, he thought. He could not wait to see the bird. He looked down on her cage from his high perch, straining to catch sight of her.

Then he saw her. Her body was green with peach markings at her throat. She had black, blue, and peach tail feathers. He looked once, and again. Could it be true? Pachuco did not know how he knew (since the Mirasol he remembered before their race through the forest with the troll at their heels was shimmering and sparkling on the dance floor in her ball gown), but he was positive that the peach-throated lovebird was none other than Mirasol herself!

The shock of recognition was too much for him. He lost his footing and took a sudden dive from his high perch to the floor of his cage. His wings fluttered loudly as he attempted to land squarely on his talons and not injure his body or wings.

He tried to hide his embarrassment as he felt the eyes of everyone in the kitchen turning toward him.

"What's wrong with you, Pachuco?" asked the old woman. "It must be the excitement of getting a roommate."

Hardly, thought Pachuco. This is Mirasol. I'm sure of it. She is the girl I've been thinking about ever since I arrived on this planet. She's the one I shared dances with at the Palace Ball and spent a terrifying night fleeing from Malvado the troll. And now it seems that Malvado has turned *both* of us into parrots. *Incredible!*

Pachuco wondered if Mirasol would recognize him and if they would be able to communicate like he had with the other Amazons in the pet shop. They were both parrots, but they were not the same variety. Would that make a difference? He would not be able to stand it if they were forced to live in cages next to each other in the old couple's kitchen and did not share a common language.

Pachuco tried to get Mirasol's attention, but she seemed drained and did not answer his calls. She drank some water, ate a few seeds, and immediately climbed to the highest perch in her cage.

"Mirasol, Mirasol," shrieked Pachuco loudly, but she stared straight ahead and did not seem to notice him. She appeared to be asleep though her eyes remained open.

"Let's let the lovebird rest after all the excitement," said the old woman, as she covered her cage with a sheet.

"I'll cover Pachuco's cage, too. Tomorrow they can get to know each other," said the old woman."

No, no, I have to talk to Mirasol, thought Pachuco. We are already acquainted, and this can't wait until tomorrow.

He shouted his most raucous call, but there was no response.

The old woman gave Pachuco a hard look as she covered his cage. "Quiet, now, Pachuco," she scolded. "Go to sleep and let the lovebird get some rest. That's enough of your carrying on for today."

Pachuco stared into the blackness as he stood on a single talon on the top perch in his cage under his sheet. He tried to stay awake.

"Mirasol is back! Mirasol is back!" the Amazon exclaimed.

She is the answer to a prayer, he thought to himself. And the second miracle he had encountered on Planet Earth.

Pachuco's little black tongue moved up and down in his beak, and he began to fall asleep. He snored softly as he lapsed into unconsciousness.

CHAPTER SEVEN

Mirasol's Adventures

The last thing Mirasol remembered was Malvado brandishing his wand over her head after he had used his black magic to triumph in the battle with Pachuco.

When she regained consciousness, she was in a nest surrounded by five chicks, all peeping and bantering in competition for tasty morsels supplied by their parents. At first she could hardly bring herself to taste the food and tried to down it whole. She could not keep herself from gagging at the sight of the partially digested insects and worms that had been alive just moments before. But soon she grew so hungry that she did not object to the brown, slimy food and even began anticipating the nourishment. Joining the fray, she opened her mouth to receive the protein.

She observed the chattering hatchlings and realized that she was a bird as well. The awareness of her transformation from a girl—a Princess at that—to a chick in a nest in the wild, somehow did not cause her too much concern. She who was so familiar with the birds on Pacifista knew that she was no longer on her home planet.

She must have miraculously traveled through space and time from her galaxy. All that mattered to her now was that she was alive.

She was confused when she compared herself to the other hatchlings. She was smaller, her beak was pointier, and her feathers were developing a color-scheme of their own in green, blue, and peach.

The other chicks had markings of brown and gray that allowed them to blend into the natural habitat of the streambed in which they lived. She hoped they would not notice her plumage. When she could, she snuggled close to the other hatchlings to hide her colorful feathers.

Mirasol befriended the two male hatchlings.

"Don't listen when the other hatchlings say your plumage is odd," said one. "What do they know about colors of feathers? You will probably find a nest where you will be in high style when you grow up."

"You may be developing more slowly than the rest of us, but that's OK," advised the other. "Just take your time, Mirasol. You are bound to become a spectacular bird."

When they were alone in the nest, one of the three female chicks spoke up, "I am going to grow up to lay the most eggs and have the most stunning nests."

A second female hatchling boasted, "I will find the most attractive mate."

The third female chick vowed, "I will make my nests in the highest branches of the cottonwood trees near the great river."

"What about you, Mirasol?" asked one of the male hatchlings. "What is your dream?"

"I have always dreamed of leaving home and having adventures," answered Mirasol before she could stop herself. She had no idea if birds ever considered having adventures.

The three female hatchlings stared at her, their pupils flaring. "This bird is talking nonsense," said one of them.

"Nothing of the sort," said one of her friends. "She is clever and will develop into an amazing bird. Mark my words!"

"I highly doubt it," said the first hatchling. "Imagine wanting to encounter more excitement than we come upon in a day. No one could possibly want that."

"Well, I'm sure we all want to be the fastest flyer," said one of the female hatchlings. "Papa always says the fastest flyer eats first."

The other hatchlings nodded their agreement. Mirasol secretly agreed with the hatchlings. Since she had learned to dance on Pacifista, she had wished that she could take to the air. She had decided that gliding in the air would be a wonderful adventure.

About a month after hatching, the day arrived for their first flying lesson. The father bird demonstrated the take-off, gliding, and landing motions.

"I expect nothing short of perfection from you hatchlings," he said.

Mirasol observed the movements and memorized how to perform them. Still, her stomach lurched when she thought about flying. Flying was a challenge she had dreamed about back in Pacifista, but now that she was about to leave the nest, she found the prospect of taking to the air frightening.

One by one the adult birds coaxed the hatchlings from the nest, and the young birds took to the air. Their initial flight was from the nest to a tree limb five feet away.

"Your take-off was too slow," the male adult bird criticized as one of the hatchlings took to the air. "Now take off and land three more times."

He reviewed the flights of all the chicks and had them repeat their performances.

As Mirasol looked on she found it difficult to decide who was the fastest flyer. They all improved as they repeated their flights.

She was the smallest and the last out of the nest. She had difficulty taking off and nearly crashed into a tree branch. She set her sights high on the umbrella of several cottonwoods. At last she launched and soared high, higher into the air. She was floating above the nest, the hatchlings, even above the treetops. She was flying hundreds of yards into the air, almost as high as the clouds! And what's more, she was moving at incredible speeds. Even hiking and folk dancing on Pacifista could not compare to this. She had no desire to return to the nest.

Mirasol had flown so much higher, faster, and farther than the hatchlings that she was confident that she had won the flying contest. She was elated and flew for a full half hour before she finally forced herself to return to the nest, expecting the admiration of all.

The young hatchlings looked at her in amazement, but the parent birds eyed her suspiciously.

"You are not one of us," the male adult bird had snarled. "You are green, blue, and peach. Who ever heard of a bird with bright feathers? And you fly like the wind. Leave this nest and never come back. You should be glad that we raised you like one of our own. Now be gone!"

Mirasol tried to hold back tears as she bade farewell to her two hatchling friends as the three other chicks and their parents looked on. She flew swiftly from the nest.

She was an able flyer but did not know how to find food or defend herself against animals or birds of prey. She was encouraged when she remembered her study of biology on Pacifista. She hoped that some of that knowledge would help her on her journey.

She could see a mountain range in the distance, and she flew toward it. It reminded her of the mountains on Pacifista. At the end of the afternoon she was in the foothills of the mountains. It was cooler there and she hoped to find water. She had encountered no water since she left the nest near the banks of the river, and she was very thirsty.

She could see no lakes or rivers from the air, so she stopped in a farmyard to rest and search for water. There on the patio of the farmhouse, several feet from where she touched down, was the largest cat she had ever seen.

The great cat was beige, and his coat had dark brown markings. His ears stood straight up and had similar dark markings at their tips. She guessed him to be forty inches long and twenty inches high. He had a short, perky tail and seemed to be at ease, lounging in the farmyard in the afternoon sunshine. She couldn't stop staring at the cat's ears; they reminded her of old-fashioned shoes with curling tips. In all, she found him to be a magnificent creature.

It occurred to her that he hardly looked like a family pet after he yawned and stretched to extend his entire body and reveal his razor-sharp claws and chiseled incisors. Mirasol imagined sketching the cat in her notebook if she had spotted him from afar on one of her hikes in Pacifista. Even as a girl she would not have wanted to meet him face to face.

When the cat's gaze lighted on Mirasol, his yellow-green eyes gleamed. He began to move ever so slowly in her direction. If she had not been staring straight at him, she might not have noticed his motion. After several minutes, he arched his back as if he were about to leap.

Mirasol realized this cat was dangerous and that she had to leave the farmyard immediately, but she was paralyzed. She could not move any part of her body, much less lift off the ground. Flying when facing life-threatening peril was not as easy as her take-off from the nest where she had hatched.

Mirasol tried again to lift off the ground, but she remained frozen. She tried once more. This time she barely managed to take off just as the great cat leaped and pawed at her. A few of her colorful tail feathers slowly settled to the earth as she flew as rapidly as she could above the cat. She heard him produce a harsh growl from deep in his throat. Mirasol flew in a zigzag pattern. She tried to calm herself and even the course of her flight by singing one of the folk songs from Pacifista that her grandmother had taught her as a child. The song was off-key but it reminded her of her Kingdom, and she managed to ascend into the afternoon glare.

She continued eastward toward the mountain range. The afternoon sun of summer was bearing down. Her thirst was intense. She knew she would have to find water if she were to survive. Mirasol spotted a stream as she approached a mountainous area and landed in a tree to survey the scene. She had learned her lesson from the great cat and was not about to touch down before observing the landscape from above.

Balancing on a tree branch, she looked below and saw a six-foot gray-brown snake with black and white rings on its tail nestled by the stream bank. She was familiar with snakes on Pacifista, but she had never seen a reptile like this. The snake was heavy-bodied with diamond-shaped blotches on its back and fainter, smaller blotches on its sides. The rear of the snake looks just like a raccoon, she thought.

She might have laughed at the sight except that just then the snake spotted her and made a sound like a rattle in a most loud and disturbing manner. It coiled its body straight up in the air and raised its head threateningly. It extended its jaw that had been tiny but suddenly looked large enough to easily swallow her whole.

Mirasol's heart was beating wildly as she flew away from the tantalizing stream, though she longed for a long taste of the fast-moving water. She was becoming aware of the reality of life in the high desert. Living with little water was an extreme hardship.

Mirasol flew on until she spotted a huge solid rectangle filled with the bluest water she had ever seen. It was surrounded by a bright green carpet of grass. Could this be a mirage, she wondered? As there was no tree overhanging the water hole, she lighted on a fence, and scouted for predators. She waited for a full fifteen minutes before deciding to fly down for a drink.

Just as she was landing on the bank of the water hole, out of some bushes came a fast-moving ground bird streaked with brown and white underparts. On its head was a shaggy brown crest. Its tail was almost the same length as its twenty-inch body. It had long tail feathers that were white-tipped on the outer edges, and its bill was long and heavy. The bird (if that indeed was what it was, Mirasol thought wryly) had the longest legs she had ever seen.

The creature approached Mirasol and began to make a gurgling sound that sounded like "Perrp, perrp, perrp." Mirasol wondered if she could communicate with it.

She asked the bird with the herringboned feathers how it was today, and if she might share a drink in its water hole.

"Absolutely not," answered the bird. "I have chicks to feed in my nest, and you look like a perfect snack for them."

"No, please sir . . . um, I mean ma'am," she begged, shifting her balance from talon to talon. "I would not make a fit snack for your family, today, believe me."

Her words appeared to make the long-legged bird annoyed with her. The last thing Mirasol wanted to do was to fly off without a drink. But somehow she sensed that the bird was bracing to rush at her. And she was right! Before she could take a gulp of water, the bird accelerated and charged at her.

Mirasol flew up to the fence surrounding the water hole. From there taking to the air was easier than lifting off from the ground.

"Why do all these wild creatures seem determined to attack me?" asked Mirasol to no one in particular. "I have done nothing to them. On Pacifista I respected all living things."

After that she did not stop until she reached a housing development in the mountains with single-story casitas sporting orange tile roofs. She lighted on a roof of one of the small houses and hung on with her talons.

She squawked because she was so tired and thirsty.

A woman with red hair came out of the house accompanied by a man. She waved a broom handle at the bird. "Quick, climb up on the roof and rescue that parakeet!" she instructed the man.

"Whatever for? Wild birds are supposed to be on the roof," he said.

"She's not a wild bird," protested the woman. "She's a parakeet. Last time I checked, tropical birds were not native to New Mexico."

"Oh, all right," her husband replied, though it was apparent he wasn't too keen on the prospect of the climb.

He dragged a ladder out of his garage and soon appeared on the roof next to Mirasol, holding a shoebox. She shrieked and tried her best to bite him, but the man was quick, and she was exhausted, so she couldn't put up much of a fight. The man put her in the box and descended the ladder as his wife looked on.

The red-headed woman punched holes in the shoebox with a shiny metallic object and put a small container of water in the box. She cut up some lettuce and grapes and put them in the box as well.

Mirasol burrowed into one corner of the box and closed her eyes, trying to erase all memories of this bewildering day.

She wished these two humans would go away. Finally the red-headed woman put the lid on the box, and the harsh afternoon sun was replaced by a soothing darkness.

Sometime later she sensed the motion of some kind of wagon. Whatever it was, it moved much faster and was far less jolting that the wagons she was accustomed to on Pacifista. She hoped that she was staying on this planet and wasn't making a leap to another planet or galaxy. She'd had enough traveling for one day.

Mirasol was exhausted, but she remembered the sensations of the vehicle stopping and someone carrying her box. When the lid of the box was removed she saw a room full of people staring at her.

She was still thirsty and finding it difficult to breathe. The water that the red-headed woman had put in the box had spilled on the journey.

Mirasol saw an older woman lift her gently into some kind of wire enclosure that was equipped with water, seeds, and perches that just fit her talons.

She heard another bird shrieking wildly near her, but she was too tired to attempt to interpret its language. She prayed the bird would not try to attack her in the night.

She drank her first taste of water since she left the banks of the large river. She drank continuously for several minutes. The water quenched her thirst and tasted as pure as the water in Pacifista's waterfalls. Then she was barely able to climb to the highest perch as the woman put a light cover over her cage.

As she fell asleep, she hoped she would not dream.

CHAPTER EIGHT

Pachuco and Mirasol Reunited

The following morning the old couple woke up early and headed for the kitchen to uncover the birds.

"*Buenos días, pajaritos verdes,*" the old man greeted the birds.

The woman first removed the sheet from the lovebird's cage. Then she uncovered the sheet from Pachuco's cage as well.

The Amazon was in full display with his wing and tail feathers fanned out revealing glorious red, blue, and black feathers. His eyes were dilating as he danced on his top perch. He was at least three times the lovebird's size.

"Well, look at him," said the old man. "He's already showing off for the little lady."

Pachuco beamed one mischievous eye at the lovebird and whistled a variation of "La Cucaracha."

Then his voice took on a more serious tone, "Mirasol, do you recognize me? I am King Pachuco from Pacifista."

"I didn't think I'd ever see you again!" exclaimed Mirasol. "I can hardly believe it's you."

"Can you understand me?" asked Pachuco, his heart skipping a beat.

"Yes, if I concentrate hard," said Mirasol. "I'm sure I'll pick up your language in a few weeks."

"I'm certain that now that we're together, we'll be able to find a way to return to Pacifista," said Pachuco as he energetically dipped his beak in his food dish and began eating his breakfast.

"I doubt it," said Mirasol, who appeared to shake her head sorrowfully. "Though I don't know precisely where we are, we seem to be far from home, and surely it's impossible that we'll be able to retrace our steps and return to Pacifista as birds. I wonder if you have any idea how difficult it is to fly cross-country on this planet. There are so many creatures waiting to devour you."

Mirasol eyed her seeds but made no move to eat the food or water the old woman had provided for her.

"Maybe we *will* return to Pacifista," said Pachuco, who was trying to speak slowly and clearly so Mirasol would understand him. He had few problems understanding her speech. "Mirasol, we have arrived here, so there's a good possibility that we will return. We have merely to make a plan and follow it."

"I'm not convinced," said Mirasol, who finally picked at her seeds and drank some water in her cage. The old woman tried to coax her into eating some of the lettuce, carrots, and radishes that she fed Pachuco, but the lovebird did not seem interested.

In the evening after Mirasol had time to rest, the couple let the birds out of their cages to stretch their wings.

"That new bird is a marvelous flyer," said the old woman after observing the lovebird gracefully take to the air.

"Compared to the lovebird's soaring, Pachuco flies like a B-52 bomber," said the old man with a laugh.

Pachuco fluffed up his wings and stared into space. He could not argue that Mirasol's tiny body and short wingspan made her a superb flyer. She floated up to the top of the curtain rods near the ceiling, and he could only crane his neck and watch her from his low-lying perch in the den.

"What's the matter, Pachuco?" teased Mirasol. "Are you jealous because I fly so effortlessly?"

I should have guessed, thought Pachuco, that a Princess who could float across the dance floor at the Palace Ball, easily performing every variety of dance, would also make an exceptional flyer. But how could he have predicted her abilities after transforming from a Princess into a peach-throated lovebird?

The second night after Mirasol came to live with them, as the old man and woman were putting the two birds to bed, the old woman asked, "What shall we call the lovebird?"

"We'll sleep on her name as well," replied the old man. "This time you choose the name."

The next morning when they awoke the old man asked his wife if a name had come to her in the night. "Yes," she replied. "She is such a small, sweet little thing, her name will be *Dulcita*."

"We will call you Dulcita from now on," the old woman told Mirasol when she uncovered her cage.

Pachuco paced on his high perch with his brown eyes flashing, and Mirasol let out a dejected shriek. Pachuco had told Mirasol how the old man had guessed his name from Pacifista, and he had hoped that the old woman would come up with her given name, too.

"Dulcita sounds like a piece of candy," she told Pachuco. "I'll show the old woman that I am far from sugar-coated!"

After that day when the couple let Mirasol out of her cage, she flew as far away from them as possible. She lighted on the highest surface she could find and made them climb on stepstools and ladders to fetch her. She searched for any open door or window to try to escape from the house.

Despite her pranks, Mirasol displayed an extraordinary talent. She began to weave. She used her tiny, sharp beak to cut the paper from the bottom of her cage into small strips. Then she carefully wove the strips through the bars in the back and sides of her cage.

When the old woman saw what she was doing, she gave her colored construction paper to work with. Soon Mirasol was weaving designs in brilliant reds, greens and yellows. When friends and family came to the old couple's kitchen, Mirasol's multi-colored weavings were the first things that caught their eyes.

"A bird that can weave!" they exclaimed. "What a sight!"

Pachuco was blue. He squawked and refused to eat his food. He was not used to being shown up by Mirasol or anyone else, for that matter. He was jealous of Mirasol's weaving as he had been resentful of her exceptional flying abilities.

He wanted to shriek, "Look at me. I can whistle 'La Cucaracha,' mimic the sounds of the telephone and the old man's razor, and fly, too. And I am King of the Kingdom of Pacifista in the next galaxy."

But he remained silent and hung his head.

"What's the matter, Pachuco?" taunted Mirasol. "Are you jealous of a Princess who's been transformed into a lovebird and remembers how to weave?"

Pachuco did not respond. He found Mirasol's teasing unkind. His emotions were sensitive; he had little experience responding to mockery, even the friendly kind.

The couple observed that Pachuco was not as lively as he had been before Mirasol's arrival.

"We have raised Pachuco as an only child," said the old woman one day. "It's too hard on him to adjust to Mirasol flying freely around the house."

"All right then," agreed the old man. "Mirasol will remain in her cage, and Pachuco will sit with us on his perch in the den. She doesn't seem to mind being cage-bound. She has become quite the little weaver."

Pachuco was more at ease when Mirasol remained in her cage, and he was allowed to fly from his cage to his perch in the den when the couple was at home. He sat with the old man and woman when they watched television and sometimes nibbled at the food on their plates when they had an evening snack. Mirasol remained quiet in her kitchen hideaway and wove to her heart's content.

When the old man and woman were out, the birds climbed to the high perches in their cages and reminisced about their life in Pacifista.

"Do you miss your life at the Royal Palace?" asked Mirasol one evening when the couple had gone to a performance at an Hispanic theater.

"Yes," said Pachuco. "Even though I had to study hard all day with my tutors on subjects ranging from calculus to literature. And I had to train in the martial arts with my coach and learn political strategy from my father's advisers. Of course, I miss my mother. She was always worrying about me, telling me to dress properly, and objecting when I insisted on wearing my running shoes to palace functions. She must have been beside herself when we disappeared the night of the Palace Ball. I wonder what she's doing now."

"What was your black Lab like, Pachuco?" Mirasol asked.

"Diamante was the best dog ever. He was all heart. He was muscular and had a massive head. Every day I would wrap a red handkerchief around his neck. He loved to hike and wrestle, and he slept at the foot of my bed," said Pachuco. "I'm sure he didn't understand when I didn't return from the Palace Ball. He must be miserable without me. I wonder who walks him now."

"I'm sure he's missing you," said Mirasol.

"Did you have pets, Mirasol?" asked Pachuco.

"No, but I liked to hike. I kept journals and sketched the animals I observed," she said. "I was a biology buff like my father."

"My father and I hunted in the fall," said Pachuco. "We would go off on trips for weeks and come back with meat for the winter."

"It must have been wonderful to have your father all to yourself," said Mirasol, who suddenly appeared downcast. "My parents died when I was very young."

"What was your life like, Mirasol, with your grandmother?" asked Pachuco.

"Life in my grandmother's castle was simple; it was nothing like your life in the Royal Palace. We wove on our loom and grew vegetables," said Mirasol. "My grandmother was an exceptional cook and made fabulous meals with the plainest of ingredients. I am getting hungry just thinking of her soups and stews. She was not an easy woman to please, but still, I find myself missing her so much."

"You will see her again soon, Mirasol," said Pachuco. "I promise."

"Pachuco, I know you believe we'll return to Pacifista," said Mirasol. "I wish I could share your hope, but Malvado is running Pacifista. Even if we could get back to Pacifista, what could we hope to accomplish as parrots?"

"If we were transformed to parrots, we can be changed back to a King and a Princess," said Pachuco. "Spells are always reversible. That's the first law of sorcery."

"I am familiar with that law," said Mirasol. "But our basic knowledge of sorcery is no match for Malvado's cunning with his magic wand. We have both seen the damage he can cause."

"If we concentrate, plan, and use all of our powers, we'll make it back to Pacifista, and we will become transformed back to the King and Princess once again," said Pachuco. "The first step is escaping from my cage. I've been working on it, and I think I've just about got it down. Look, Mirasol!"

Using his beak and one talon, Pachuco fiddled with his food tray. He was able to free his head, but the rest of his large body remained in the cage.

Mirasol seemed to try to hold it back, but she let out a snicker that came out like a low shriek.

"Well, I haven't perfected the technique yet," Pachuco admitted. "But it's coming. Don't laugh, Mirasol. We *will* return to our homeland in Pacifista. I'll see the Queen and Diamante, and you'll see your grandmother. We will both see the rainbows kaleidoscoping at sunset and the waterfalls with their cascading bands of color.

"You have to believe. It won't happen unless you believe," continued Pachuco, who eyed her wistfully.

Mirasol was silent. She closed her eyes and stood on one talon from the highest perch in her cage.

Pachuco knew Mirasol was still recovering from her travel in the wild from the river to the mountains. She was bound to become more optimistic about their trip back to their homeland when she was fully recovered. He knew her to be an intelligent and resourceful girl, and he was sure she would be an asset to him in planning the voyage once she was rested.

As he was falling asleep that night surrounded by the blackness under his sheet, Pachuco was certain he heard Mirasol whisper, "I don't care what Pachuco says. I know my dreams are as close as I will ever come to returning to Pacifista's shores."

We'll see about that, thought Pachuco, as he made his snoring sound and lapsed into sleep.

CHAPTER NINE

The Grandchildren Arrive

O ne morning in late summer the couple came into the kitchen for breakfast. They uncovered the birds, and Pachuco noticed a gleam in the old man's eye and a bounce in the old woman's step. When the couple hastily dispensed with breakfast and began cooking enchilada casseroles, green chile stew, and *chiles rellenos*, he knew it was far from an ordinary day. In fact, from the amount of food the old man and woman were preparing, he was beginning to think that whatever was going to happen might go on for weeks.

Pachuco's suspicions were confirmed when he observed the old woman preparing what she told the old man was a *pastel de chocolate tres leches*. She rarely baked, but today she put the batter for a white cake in the oven. When it was done, she let it cool and then poked holes in top of the cake. Into the cake she poured melted chocolate, condensed and evaporated milk, and sour cream that she blended in a machine that *whirred* loudly. Finally she covered the cake with whipped cream. Pachuco's eyes were bulging.

"I want some of that," he squawked.

"*Calmate, Pachuco,*" responded the old woman, putting the cake in the refrigerator.

"Tomorrow we will have to go to the airport to pick up the grandchildren. They'll be arriving from California at 9:00 a.m.," said the old man, when the couple took a break from their preparations and sat down at the kitchen table for a cup of coffee. "We'll have to set the alarm clock so we don't oversleep."

"We haven't seen them in a year," said the old woman. "Veronica will be eleven years old and Marc will be twelve now. I can't wait to see how they've changed. Veronica has been taller than Marc almost since she was a toddler. I wonder if Marc has grown."

So that's it, thought Pachuco. Two grandchildren are coming for a visit. He looked over at Mirasol in her cage. She seemed unaware of the flurry of activity around her in the kitchen as she cut slivers of construction paper and continued to weave the colorful tapestry through the bars in the back of her cage.

"Mirasol," called Pachuco. "We're having a visit from the couple's grandchildren tomorrow. The food will be fantastic for weeks."

"I'm not impressed," said Mirasol. "I don't enjoy that kind of food like you do."

"I know," said Pachuco. "But the children may be fun to play with.

The next morning the couple came into the kitchen to awaken the birds. It was earlier than the usual time, and Pachuco protested loudly. He tried to nip at the old man's fingers as he inserted his feeding tray full of cut-up carrots, bananas, green pepper and bits of scrambled egg.

"Well, look here," said the old man. "Take it easy, Pachuco, we're rushed because we have to leave for the airport in a few minutes."

The old man and woman ate a hasty breakfast and took off for the airport in their truck. The truck made a wheezing and sputtering sound that Pachuco and Mirasol recognized when it was down the block.

The birds finished eating and climbed back up to their top perches to nap. This might be the last time we have to relax in weeks, thought Pachuco as he tucked his beak between his wing feathers and closed his eyes.

An hour later they heard the truck approaching the house and the garage door opening. Then they heard two sets of swiftly running feet followed by the familiar strides of the old man and woman. The back door swung open and the children raced into the kitchen.

"The birds are beautiful!" exclaimed Veronica. "Look at their brightly colored feathers! And the little one has a weaving across the back of her cage. Can they come out of their cages?"

"Yes," agreed Marc. "I want to hold them."

"Relax a minute and get settled," said the old man. "I'll take your suitcases to your rooms. The birds will need time to adjust to you. They have never met children before. Dulcita doesn't come out of her cage, but Pachuco can."

The children unpacked their suitcases and returned to the kitchen for lunch. They ate large portions of enchilada casserole and chiles rellenos, fried green chiles filled with white Mexican cheese. Pachuco, of course, ate these dishes as well and made a clicking sound with his tongue on his beak to show that he was thoroughly enjoying them.

"Marc, I can't believe it, but you are taller than your sister," said the old woman. "And your voice is lower as well. You are becoming a young man."

"And you are becoming an attractive young lady, Veronica," said the old man. The children seemed embarrassed at the talk about their appearance. Marc changed the subject.

"Can Pachuco come out of his cage now?" he asked.

"I don't know how he will react to you. He's timid with strangers at first. But we'll give it a try," said the old man.

The old man released the steel bar that held Pachuco's cage shut. Once he had done this, Pachuco was able to maneuver his beak on the cage door to open it.

"Look!" Marc exclaimed. "This bird is smart."

Pachuco climbed to the top of his cage. He was full from the lunch and might have enjoyed another nap, but he had few opportunities to leave the cage during the day, so he decided to make the most of it.

The old man lifted Pachuco out of his cage and held him for several minutes. Marc and Veronica started playing tag and took off down a long hall in the ranch-style house.

Where are they going, wondered Pachuco, who had never done much exploring in the house. The old couple did not allow him to roam further than his territory, which was the kitchen, the den, and one of the bathrooms.

When the children returned—breathless—to the kitchen, the old man shifted Pachuco to the boy's shoulder. Pachuco walked from one of the child's shoulders to the other. Marc knelt down to give Pachuco space to roam on his back. Pachuco took a liking to the boy and remained on his shoulder even when Marc and Veronica continued to run through the house.

"Not too fast," cautioned the old woman, "Pachuco is not used to people running with him."

"We'll be careful," promised Veronica. "And I want my turn next."

The two took off with the bird in tow, running for about ten minutes. Then the old man stepped in and rescued Pachuco. "It's time for him to return to his cage," said the old man. "He needs a break."

"But what about my turn?" protested Veronica.

"You'll have to wait until tomorrow," answered her grandfather. "The parrot needs to rest now."

Pachuco was thrilled. "That was great," he reported to Mirasol once he had settled back in his cage. "You should try it."

"No, thanks," she replied. "Just watching you is enough for me. Were we like that as children on Pacifista?"

"I think so," recalled Pachuco. "I was always racing around the Palace in my favorite old sneakers with Diamante at my side. My mother was constantly telling me to slow down."

"My grandmother was always trying to slow me down, too," said Mirasol. "She said it wasn't proper for a young lady, especially a member of the Royal Court, to hurry so. When I was outdoors on my nature walks, I liked to run on the trails, but I had to slow down or I'd miss the birds and animals I liked to sketch."

"You should come out of your cage and play with the children," advised Pachuco. "They are lots of fun. What ever happened to the girl from Pacifista who wanted to have adventures instead of sitting at her loom all day long?"

"I do long for adventure," said Mirasol. "But I guess I'm still resting from my journey among the wild creatures."

One afternoon Veronica stood silently in front of the birdcages. She appeared to be studying the two birds closely as they rested on a single talon digesting their lunch. After several minutes, she exclaimed, "Pachuco, you are the King. Dulcita, you are the Princess."

Upon hearing her words Pachuco launched into a full wing and tail feather display and began shrieking wildly. Mirasol tottered on the highest perch in her cage.

"This child understands that Mirasol and I are more than an Amazon parrot and a lovebird," he squawked. "She is the most insightful human I have met on Planet Earth. If only I could talk with her!"

"Did you hear that, Mirasol?" he called. "This child knows that I am the King and you are the Princess."

"Yes, I heard what Veronica said, but how could she know you are the King and I'm the Princess?" asked Mirasol. "It must be some kind of coincidence."

Marc had been passing through the kitchen and had overheard Veronica talking to the birds.

"Pachuco is a parrot, and Dulcita is a lovebird, Veronica. That's it," he said. "Act your age."

"You believe what you want to believe," responded Veronica, "but I know what I know."

"You're impossible," said Marc and went out to the backyard to help his grandfather strip some wood for a carving they were working on. He allowed the door to slam behind him.

Veronica looked after her brother and shook her head. "Why does he never believe me when I can tell something is not how it seems?" she asked as the birds looked on. "He has no imagination!"

She looked at the birds fondly and breathed a deep sigh.

"I wish I could help you return to your homeland," said Veronica. "But I don't even know where you're from."

Pachuco squawked. He knew she didn't understand, but her knowledge that they were more than birds was a great comfort to him.

The next morning Pachuco heard the old couple and the children talking about traveling to the west side of the city to shop in a Mexican *mercado*. "You will love it," said the old man who had been born in the interior of Mexico. "There are bright decorations everywhere and you can buy every kind of Mexican product. And they have a meat market that sells Mexican cuts of meat you've never tasted, like *barbacoa* and tongue."

The children were eager to explore the market. The old woman finished the breakfast dishes, and they piled into the truck.

"I wonder if they will bring any of the food home for me," said Pachuco who was putting on weight with all the treats the grandchildren were sneaking to him. He hoped he would still be able to climb to his highest perch to go to sleep. He feared the old couple would discover his weight gain and put him on a strict diet.

When the foursome returned, they carried five grocery bags filled with delicacies. The children were excited about their trip to the mercado.

"There was loud *mariachi* music as we approached the market," said Veronica to the birds. "Inside were crowds of people with newborn babies and young children piled into the baskets with the groceries."

"Look, Pachuco," said Marc. "We stopped to have a snack of *carne asada* on hand-made tortillas with blackened jalapeño peppers. We ate at picnic tables. I brought you back a taste."

He took out a mini-sized taco of grilled beef that he had stored in his jeans pocket in a napkin and put it in Pachuco's food dish.

Pachuco buried his beak in the taco, and he clicked his tongue on his beak, his sound of contentment. He devoured every bit of the tiny taco. From the corner of his eye, he could see Mirasol looking on without emotion.

The children also removed from one of the bags a supply of *paletas*, Mexican popsicles, made with tropical fruit like pineapple, coconut, mango, jicama, and papaya. Veronica gave Pachuco a taste of her mango paleta, and he ate it merrily.

"Pachuco, Grandfather was right," said Marc. "It must be just like Mexico. There were all varieties of *pan mexicano*, all types of meat, vegetables, Mexican cheeses, hand-made tortillas, a whole assortment of fish, and even a large supply of *piñatas* dangling from the ceiling. There were household goods and even jewelry for sale."

"There were fans with swirling colored crepe paper everywhere," said Veronica. "You would have loved it, Dulcita."

"And the prices are the best of any market in town," said the old woman. "We go there to stock up whenever we can."

"And don't forget the fruit juices. There were watermelon, pineapple, and papaya juices," said Marc. "What wonderful flavors! We've never tasted anything like them!"

The old man was about to bite into a *tuna*, a cactus fruit, and several types of Mexican candies.

"Let's give a taste of one of the candies to Pachuco," said Veronica. "He would love it."

"No way," said the old man. "The *dulcitas* are pure sugar. They are not for birds."

The foursome was soon wolfing down *empanadas de crema* with coffee and milk. Veronica snuck Pachuco a chunk of the Mexican bread when the old couple was not looking.

How will I ever lose weight and return to Pacifista? Pachuco wondered. With the children filling my food dish, I am putting on ounces every day. He wondered if Mirasol was aware he was eating more than ever.

Mirasol seemed to eye Pachuco warily, but she said nothing that evening when the old woman covered them with their sheets.

Pachuco whistled a jaunty tune before he snored briefly and fell into a contented slumber.

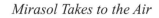

CHAPTER TEN

Mirasol Takes to the Air

O ne morning after breakfast, Mirasol was engaging in her customary activity, shredding colored paper with her tiny pointed beak. Then she skillfully wove the thin strips of paper in and out of the bars in the back of her cage. The weaving was almost effortless; she had been maneuvering the paper with her beak in this manner since she arrived at the house of the old couple weeks before.

This weaving is getting to be a mindless task, she admitted to herself. On Pacifista she had found weaving at her loom tiresome at times, but at least she and Lupita produced brilliant ceiling-to-floor-length tapestries for the walls of their castle, practical clothing, and spectacular ball gowns. What was all her effort producing on Earth? Nothing more than a woven multi-colored backdrop for her cage. Yes, visitors to the house admired it, but she was tiring of their attention.

Veronica had stationed herself in front of Mirasol's cage. "Dulcita, you need some excitement in your life," she said as she removed the bar fastening the lovebird's cage.

"Fly! Exercise those wings! Take off!" she exclaimed.

Mirasol glanced over to view Pachuco snoozing on the top perch of his cage. Marc and his grandfather were in the backyard chopping wood for the winter. The old woman was nowhere to be seen.

Well, why not? thought Mirasol. I haven't been out of my cage in weeks, not even on the day each week the old man cleaned it.

Mirasol slowly climbed to the top of her cage as Veronica looked on.

"Go for it, Dulcita," Veronica encouraged her. "You shouldn't be shut up in your cage like a prisoner."

"You're right," shrieked Mirasol, as she lifted off from the cage. She had forgotten how astonishing it felt to take off and soar through the air.

She made several tours of the house.

Because the children were staying in rooms off a long hallway in the rear of the house, she explored that area and noticed the children's suitcases and clothes strewn all over their rooms.

It reminds me of my room in my castle in Pacifista, thought Mirasol. My grandmother was always reminding me to straighten up. Even the memory of her grandmother's scolding filled her with longing.

Still, she thought, Veronica and Marc seem far less mature than she and Pachuco on Pacifista. And we are the same ages as they are!

Veronica ran after the lovebird, though she could barely keep up with her.

"Slow down, Dulcita, I'm way behind you," she called out. "If I lose you, we'll both be in trouble!"

Mirasol did not pay attention to her advice. She was finally free of the bars of her cage, and she was going to make the most of it. She flew on, circling the ranch house and looking for a way to escape to the outdoors. She longed to rise above the trees and approach the clouds again. There was nothing like the rush of skyrocketing through the air unrestrained by any obstacles.

She did not think about the animals in the wild that might attack her. She focused solely on the enormous pleasure she took in flying.

Just then Mirasol noticed that the back door was opening. The old man was coming in from wood chopping in the yard. Mirasol escaped through the open door. Veronica was following on the run, two rooms behind her.

"Who let Dulcita out of her cage?" shouted the old man who reversed his direction like a practiced basketball player and headed out to the back porch after Mirasol.

Mirasol had bumped the old man's shoulder as she took off out the door. The force of the encounter stunned her tiny body and threw her to the ground just beyond the porch. She was beginning to recover and was about to take off and climb into the turquoise New Mexico skies.

The old man swiftly grabbed her and wrapped his stout fingers around her talons. He whisked her off the ground in seconds.

Mirasol was surprised by his quickness despite his age and powerful body build.

"Dulcita, let's get you back in your cage," the old man said. "We can't risk losing you."

He brought the lovebird back into the kitchen, put her in her cage, and fastened it securely.

Mirasol was frustrated that her plan to soar and glide in the wild had failed. This ranch house with its nine-foot ceilings did not provide her with a challenge when it came to flying.

"I never got an answer to my question," the old man roared. "Whoever let Dulcita out of her cage had better come to the kitchen now!"

Veronica appeared, her head held low. "I did," she said. "Dulcita needed the exercise, and she was miserable in her cage. She had to get out."

"Why didn't you ask me or your grandmother before you let her fly free?" demanded the old man. "She could have escaped through a door or window, and we could have lost her. Did you ever think about that?"

"No, I guess not," said Veronica.

"If you want to take her out again, make sure you ask permission, and let everyone in the house know what you're going to do. Dulcita flies much faster than you or Marc can run. She's a lot faster than Pachuco, and she's a lot less tame."

Mirasol observed that Marc had come in from the back yard. He towered over Veronica and said, "For such a 'bird whisperer' that wasn't a smart move."

"I made a mistake," she told her brother. "You don't need to rub it in."

The commotion over Mirasol's unsuccessful escape attempt had awakened Pachuco. "What were you thinking, Mirasol?" he shrieked. "You can't take off into the skies. We will never get back to Pacifista without both of us working on the plans. How many times have I told you this?"

"Give me a break, Pachuco," answered Mirasol. "Pacifista is in the next galaxy, and we are here. You've been enjoying yourself for weeks. How can you object to my having a little fun?"

"You don't understand, Mirasol," said Pachuco, ruffling his feathers. "There's a lot more at stake than having fun. We must return to Pacifista in the next few weeks. My Kingdom is being destroyed by the reign of Malvado the troll. We cannot delay our return to Pacifista."

"I know that, Pachuco," said Mirasol, "but I needed to feel the air flowing past my wings again."

"Look, Mirasol," Pachuco insisted. "I am the King of Pacifista, and I must fight to recapture my land. Your grandmother Lupita needs your help in your castle. And we need to work together on a plan so we can return safely to our home planet."

"Good grief, Pachuco," said Mirasol, "When will you get off this kick that we're going to go back to Pacifista?"

"Never," was Pachuco's firm answer. "We only have a short window of time to return."

Pachuco was preening his feathers as he spoke. His head disappeared between his back feathers. He was molting as fall was on the way. Now more than ever he had to tend to his feathers to keep them in order.

After the children had gone to bed that night, Mirasol heard the old man and woman discussing her near-tragic flight.

"I guess we'll have to let Dulcita out of her cage once in a while," said the old woman. "Keeping her in the cage all the time is too much for her. She's getting cabin fever."

"Yes," agreed the old man. "But we have to make sure that no one enters or leaves the house while she's flying free. If the door opens a crack, she can manage to push her way out, and she'll be lost to us forever."

Mirasol heard this conversation. It made her proud that her craftiness in trying to escape caused the old couple concern. No, they could not supply her with colored construction paper and keep her cooped up in her cage night and day. She had to fly free now and again, even if it were only in the house.

After Mirasol's failed attempt to escape from the house, her behavior was never the same. She did not give up weaving altogether, but she spent less and less time on the activity. Her weaving was sometimes colorful and balanced as it had been before, but at other times she created rumpled works with tiny pieces of paper sticking out in all directions. The old woman continued to give her construction paper in rainbow colors, but often it went untouched at the bottom of her cage.

"It's fine with me if Dulcita flies free in the house now," announced the old woman to her husband the following morning. "But you need to supervise her when she's out of the cage. Veronica and Marc are not experienced enough with birds to watch her."

The next morning when the old man and Veronica let Mirasol out of her cage, she landed on the old woman's shoulder. The old woman was seated at the kitchen table sipping coffee and eating a cinnamon roll.

"That's a nice bird, Dulcita," she said, "coming to visit me this morning."

Mirasol reached her beak up to the old woman's ear and nipped her ear lobe until blood flowed. She could not put into words why she had bitten the old woman. Her ear was convenient and seemed tender.

The old woman let out a howl of pain. "The bird has bitten me on the ear!" she screamed. "It's more painful then when I got my ears pierced years ago," she continued after a few seconds. "She packs a wallop for such a small one."

The old man laughed. "I've heard bites from a lovebird are supposed to be painful, though I've never been bitten. Dulcita is so small and silent. It's hard to imagine her inflicting a painful bite."

The old woman ran to put antiseptic on her ear lobe. "Put her back in her cage. She should not be rewarded for biting."

"But Grandpa," objected Veronica, "she just left her cage."

"No," said the old man. "Your grandmother is right. Dulcita should not be allowed to associate flying free with biting. That is not the proper way to train a bird."

The old man deposited Mirasol back in her cage. The lovebird did not know why she had bitten the old woman who was, after all, the one who fed her most mornings. Something had come over her. She would have to be more careful in the future or she would never be allowed to leave her cage.

"Mirasol, why did you bite the old woman?" squawked Pachuco, who had witnessed the incident. "You were a Princess on Pacifista. We are not aggressive people. How could you do such a thing?"

"I can't explain it, Pachuco," answered Mirasol. "Something overpowering took control of me. Maybe I'm turning into a true lovebird."

"That's not it at all, Mirasol," said Pachuco. "You are still the spirited Princess that I knew on Pacifista."

Though Pachuco's words reassured Mirasol, she had doubts. She liked the old couple who cared for her and Pachuco so well. Why had she tried to escape from the house; why had she bitten the old woman? She did not know the answer to these questions, but they bothered her as she sat in her cage on her highest perch. Now that she no longer spent so much time weaving, she had lots of time to wonder why she had behaved so oddly.

Veronica continued to station herself in front of Mirasol's cage each morning. She told the lovebird what the family had planned for the day and tried to encourage her grandfather to let Mirasol roam freely through the house. Some days she was successful in freeing Mirasol from her cage; other days she was not.

Mirasol, for her part, tried to be polite and cooperative. She worried that she would bite someone or head for an open door or window and try to escape. She still enjoyed flying indoors, but the old man watched her closely, and she knew it was unlikely that she would ever break out of the house and soar in the wild again. She felt like a prisoner confined to the house.

One afternoon Veronica stood in front of the lovebird's cage and asked her, "How would you like to come live with me and Marc in California?"

Mirasol could hardly believe her ears. Maybe she would not have to part with her friend Veronica after all. She knew Veronica was leaving soon, and she dreaded her departure.

"You could live in your cage in my room, and I'd run with you when you flew all over the house," promised Veronica. "Our house is big, and we don't have any other pets."

Later that afternoon Veronica sat down with her grandparents as they were drinking coffee in the kitchen.

"Wouldn't it be a great idea if Dulcita came back to California with me and Marc?" suggested Veronica. "She would get lots of attention, and you could spend more time with Pachuco, and he wouldn't be jealous of her. She would have to travel in a carrying case on the plane, but she's a very small bird, so that wouldn't be a problem." Veronica was flushed with excitement as she explained her idea.

"It sounds like you've been planning this for some time," said the old man. "But traveling by air can be very traumatic for any bird, especially a tiny lovebird."

"Does that mean you won't let me take her?" asked Veronica. Her cheeks were crimson.

The old man and the old woman exchanged glances.

"I'm afraid so," said the old man. "You'll have to be content to play with her when you visit us."

Veronica held back tears. "Maybe I can convince my parents to buy me a lovebird like Dulcita," she said. "My birthday is coming up next month."

Mirasol heard the exchange between Veronica and her grandparents. Veronica was the only person who had talked to her every day and lifted her spirits when she was lost in her weaving. She was the one who had reminded her of her love of flying. Mirasol almost wished the old couple had given their permission for her to accompany Veronica and Marc to California, though she had no knowledge where such a place was and what was involved in traveling there. The journey to California might turn out to be as difficult as the one to Pacifista. And where would she be then?

Besides, she owed some allegiance to Pachuco. They didn't always see eye to eye, but he had tried to reason with her when she had tried to escape. And he had tried to reassure her when she had had bitten the old woman. After all their adventures, he seemed like an old friend, even though the actual time she had known him would only add up to a matter of months.

She glanced over at the Lilac-headed Amazon who sat on a single talon on the top perch of his cage with his eyes half closed. His little black tongue moved up and down against his beak, making a snoring sound.

She would miss Veronica, she decided, who was her first true human friend. But now that she had thought about it, she could never leave Pachuco. He needed her. He was a dreamer, and if they were ever going to return to Pacifista, and she was far from convinced that this was more than a remote possibility, he would need her powers of observation and practicality. She could not imagine his successful return to their Kingdom in the next galaxy without her.

CHAPTER ELEVEN

The Final Days of the Grandchildren's Visit

One early morning, Pachuco heard the swift footsteps of the grandchildren's bare feet entering the kitchen. When Veronica and Marc had removed the birds' sheets, Pachuco began to stretch his wings, and Mirasol did the same.

"They are doing bird yoga," observed Veronica.

"They're just getting the kinks out of their wings," said Marc. "Birds don't do yoga!"

"Grandma and Grandpa must be sleeping in. Let's make breakfast for Pachuco and Dulcita," said Veronica.

"That's a great idea," agreed Marc. "We've seen Grandma give Dulcita her seeds and cut up Pachuco's vegetables. It will be a snap."

Veronica took Mirasol's food dish out of her cage and washed it. Marc removed Pachuco's dish and washed it as well. Veronica filled

Dulcita's dish high with birdseed, and then he and Veronica set about filling Pachuco's dish with vegetables and fruit. They set the birds' dishes in their cages.

Just then the old couple stumbled into the kitchen, stifling yawns.

"What's going on here?" asked the old man. "You are feeding the birds enough food for a week!"

"We are? Well, we'll just have to put some of it back," said Veronica as she poured half Mirasol's seeds back into their sack.

Pachuco had started chomping down on his green grapes, sliced radishes, bananas, apples, and carrots. As Marc tried to pull Pachuco's feeding dish out of his cage, Pachuco shrieked wildly and lunged at Marc's fingers.

"What's he trying to do?" said Marc loudly.

"You've invaded his space while he's eating, never a good idea for any animal," said the old man. "We'll have to let him have all that food today, but let me tell you how we feed him in case you want to give him his breakfast tomorrow."

The old man instructed the children to put small pieces of carrots, green pepper, banana, and a single grape in Pachuco's first feeding dish. When he had eaten those, they could add bits of scrambled egg. Finally they could add pieces of apple to the first dish and his sunflower seeds and peanuts to his second dish.

"Apples are his favorite, and he'll eat those and nothing else if he has the chance," explained the old woman. "His seeds are his candy. He gets those last and in small amounts."

"You sure have Pachuco's routine down," said Veronica, observing the sleek green bird. "If I die and go to heaven, I want to come back as Pachuco. He has all the food he could ever want laid out before him in the order he should eat it."

Pachuco bristled. First, he had almost bitten Marc, a boy he clearly liked. He couldn't explain his action. Then, he was offended by Veronica's observation that it was wonderful that all his food was set out for him in the order that it was to be consumed. If she only knew that as King of Pacifista he feasted every day on a spectacular menu, and he was the one determining what he ate and the order in which he ate it. And now Veronica claimed that she wanted to be reborn as a Lilac-headed Amazon. None of this was making any sense.

I'm beginning to understand how Mirasol felt when she tried to escape and when she bit the old woman, thought Pachuco. Maybe we are in danger of turning into birds and forgetting our past as a King and a Princess.

With breakfast concluded, Veronica and Marc dashed off to dress as the family was leaving for an outing to a water park. The children had talked about this event for days and were loud and unruly as they piled into the truck.

As soon as the truck pulled out of the garage and the garage door closed, Pachuco called out to Mirasol, who was dozing on her perch. "Mirasol, we have to talk."

"Oh, let me be, Pachuco," said Mirasol lazily. "You're not going to go on about returning to Pacifista, are you?"

"Yes, I am," said Pachuco. "We have to leave this house and this planet in the next few weeks before fall sets in."

"Pachuco, I hate to remind you of this," said Mirasol, "but you haven't even figured out how to escape from your cage. And now that you've put on weight with the grandchildren's visit, getting out of your cage will be even more of a problem."

"I didn't know you'd noticed my weight gain," admitted Pachuco, scratching his head with one talon. "I will slim down once the grandchildren leave. And I think I've figured out how to escape from my cage."

"You have?" asked Mirasol. "Then why don't you try it?"

"I don't want the old couple to know that I can break out of my cage or they will reinforce the gate. Then I'll really have trouble getting out."

"OK, once you're out of the cage, then what? Intergalactic travel is not an everyday event for a parrot and a lovebird," said Mirasol. "Just how are we going to pull this off?"

Mirasol ruffled her feathers and edged closer to Pachuco's cage. She seemed to be curious about Pachuco's strategy for space travel in spite of herself.

"I've given some thought to the theory behind our return to Pacifista while I've been cooped up in this cage," said Pachuco. "I had a wonderful astronomy teacher at the Palace on Pacifista, and he taught me all about wormholes. Do you know what wormholes are, Mirasol?"

"Sure I do," Mirasol answered. "I saw them all the time on my nature walks on Pacifista. They're not easy to spot, but you can catch the worms nosing out of their holes in the ground if you're quiet and pay close attention."

"I'm not talking about wormholes in nature!" scoffed Pachuco. "I'm talking about wormholes in astronomy. Do you know about those?'

"No," admitted Mirasol. "But you don't have to get all huffy about it. My grandmother never taught me astronomy. She didn't think that subject was necessary or fitting for a young woman of the Royal Court."

"Listen up, then," said Pachuco. "What we have to do is to create a time warp. One way to do that is with a wormhole. A wormhole in astronomy is a tube of space-time connecting two distant regions in space."

"Are you making this up?" asked Mirasol. "I've never heard of anything like a wormhole in space."

"Of course I'm not making this up!" squawked Pachuco. "Only by traveling through a wormhole can you go faster than the speed of light."

"Even if we could leave this house, how could we find the right wormhole?" asked Mirasol, who had abandoned her weaving and hopped over as close to Pachuco's cage as possible. She leaned her tiny body towards the Amazon.

"The wormhole we used to travel here will have an energy marker showing the direction that we've passed through," said Pachuco. "Once we get to it we'll know it's the one."

"What's an energy marker?" asked Mirasol.

"It's something significant left by the first travelers in the wormhole," said Pachuco. "The wormhole must be the way Malvado brought us from Pacifista to Earth. I'm sure of it, Mirasol!"

"Don't forget, Pachuco," warned Mirasol, "dealing with the creatures of New Mexico while we head towards wormholes in space will be no easy task. You were raised in a pet shop and have lived in a house. You've had an easy life. I was hatched in the wild and encountered all sorts of creatures who were trying to devour me."

"I have heard your stories, Mirasol," said Pachuco as one of his multi-colored tail feathers fluttered to the bottom of his cage. "But we have to go. There's no other way. And soon, too. Before the first frost. We'll talk more about the journey before the day of our departure."

"I still think your plan is far-fetched," said Mirasol, "but if it is to succeed you are going to need my help."

"That would be great," said Pachuco, relieved that she was finally taking some interest in their return to Pacifista. "You can think about what I've told you and make sure it sounds logical. You can also come up with plans for defending ourselves against birds and animals that may attack us in the wild. I'm reviewing all my astronomy equations in my head. It gives me something to do while I preen my feathers and play with the children."

"I'll think about my biology observations and those of my father that I've read," said Mirasol. "We'll have to use all our knowledge from Pacifista on this voyage."

Just then the birds heard the truck approaching from down the street. As it turned into the driveway, they climbed to the top perches of their cages and pretended to be napping.

The children ran into the kitchen, soaked from head to foot from the water slide. Pools of water dripped from their feet onto the worn linoleum floor.

"It was fabulous, Pachuco," raved Marc.

"It was great," said Veronica as she stood in front of Dulcita's cage. "You would have liked dipping your short feathers in the cool water."

Doubtful, thought Pachuco to himself, those torrents of water would wash Mirasol away. Even I couldn't withstand that much water pressure. What were these children thinking?

"Veronica and Marc," said the old woman, "head for the showers and change your clothes. You have goose-bumps all up and down your arms and legs."

"Do we have to, Grandma?" asked Veronica.

"Yes," said the old woman firmly. "We don't want you catching cold. You're going home tomorrow. What would your mother say if you came home sick?"

"Oh, all right," said Veronica, and she and Marc dashed off.

Pachuco saw the old man and woman pour themselves tall glasses of sun tea, tea brewed in a large container in the backyard by the sun's rays. He observed them taking the glasses of iced tea and *bizcochitos* to the back porch where she could hear them conversing as they had their snack.

The old woman crunched contentedly on one of the shortbread cookies flavored with anise and cinnamon and sipped her tea.

When the couple heard the children returning to the kitchen, the old man called to them.

"Come have some iced tea and cookies with us," the old woman sang out as well. "We're watching the humming birds and the common yellow-throated warblers. The hummers have been here since spring, but the yellowthroats with their lemon plumage are newcomers. Their appearance means that fall is coming."

"That's OK," said Marc. "We're going to take Pachuco out of his cage for a run."

Veronica and Marc were doing more than running with Pachuco. They were repeating words to him over and over.

Veronica whispered, *"Pachuquito batito, oh yeah, oh yeah, oh yeah, oh yeah!"*

Then Marc picked up the chant as he put Pachuco on Veronica's shoulder and the two dashed down the hall.

The children reappeared several times with Pachuco on their shoulders, repeating the phrase, but Pachuco did not respond. He was listening to the children and enjoying the surge of energy as they ran down the hall as the late afternoon sunlight streamed in through the windows. He lightly balanced on their shoulders with his talons. The experience was not as dramatic as the rush of flying, but he found it pleasant to be part of the smooth and rapid movement of their bare feet on the hardwood floors.

Later that afternoon the old man and woman decided to change their dinner menu from New Mexican or Mexican fare to pizza since it was the last night of the grandchildren's stay.

The children were excited. "Pizza is absolutely our favorite food," exclaimed Veronica.

Veronica and Marc took off with their grandfather to pick up a large pizza crammed with pepperoni, sausage and vegetable toppings like onions, green peppers, and chives. When they returned home with the large box, Pachuco fanned out his tail feathers as he whiffed the aroma coming from the box.

This aroma is enchanting, thought Pachuco. I know whatever is in the box will taste incredible!

The children opened the pizza box, and Pachuco's pupils flared. "I have to try some of that!" he squawked.

"Remember, Pachuco, you've got to start watching your weight," said Mirasol.

"Tomorrow," said Pachuco, "when the children have gone home."

Veronica and Marc settled down to eat and then realized that Pachuco's dish was empty. Before the old man and woman could cut Pachuco a small piece of pizza, Marc put an entire slice in his food dish. It did not fit, but Pachuco began to gorge himself on the pizza and made his happy sound with his beak against his black tongue.

He had never tasted such a combination of meat and vegetables with the addition of a zesty sauce. This is much more than fabulous, he thought, as he inserted his beak into the pizza slice. He shrieked with delight.

"This bird is going to be sick," predicted the old woman. "That is entirely too much food for an Amazon parrot."

"Let him be," said the old man. "He is enjoying himself."

The family finished the pizza. Pachuco consumed his portion as well.

Suddenly Pachuco screeched at the top of his lungs, *"Pachuquito batito, oh yeah, oh yeah, oh yeah, oh yeah!"*

The couple and the children turned to look at Pachuco, who was frantically repeating the phrase *"Oh, yeah"* with no desire or ability to stop. His raspy voice echoed throughout the house.

"Who taught him to say 'Oh yeah!'?" asked the old man.

"I did," said Marc.

"And so did I," smiled Veronica. "All the time we were racing around the house with Pachuco on our shoulders, we were teaching him those words. We wanted to surprise you."

"I had no idea that he would pick the phrase up so soon!" exclaimed Marc.

"Well, it certainly is a surprise," said the old man. "To my knowledge, Pachuco has never talked before, except to me and your grandmother. And then only on rare occasions."

"I'll have to put Pachuco to bed if he keeps up his squawking," said the old woman. "His heart must be racing and his eyes look like they are going to pop out of his head. This can't be good for him!"

Finally the Amazon settled down and the kitchen was quiet again.

The children appeared stunned by Pachuco's performance.

Pachuco was shocked by his performance as well. Why couldn't I stop saying, "Oh yeah?" he wondered. I lost control. Something came over me, and I could not stop repeating those words.

"Now you know how I felt when I tried to escape from the house and bit the old woman," said Mirasol.

Mirasol is right, he thought. We will soon become a true parrot and lovebird if we remain in our cages in the old couple's home. As much as I love the old man and woman, the grandchildren, and all the fabulous food, we must return to Pacifista. Or we risk losing our identities as a King and a Princess.

"I never would have guessed that his voice would sound so rough!" said Veronica.

"What have we done to the bird?" jested Marc. "He was so peaceful when we came, and now look at him."

"I think I will put the birds to bed early tonight," said the old woman. "They've had a big day today."

She proceeded to cover them with their sheets.

"And you two have to go to bed at a decent hour, too," said the old man. "Tomorrow we will all have to get up early to go to the airport. And you will have to keep your wits about you to arrive home safely in California on the plane. It's a long trip for two youngsters. You have a stopover in Phoenix, and you'll have to get on the light rail to make your connecting flight."

"Grandpa, please," protested Marc. "If we arrived here safely, we'll be able to return safely."

Pachuco was alert, listening to this conversation under his sheet. "Yes," he shrieked. "That's my point exactly. We came from Pacifista, not California, wherever that is, and we'll be able to return to our home."

"Did you hear, Mirasol? These two children agree with me! We *will* be able to return to Pacifista," he called out loudly.

She did not respond. She was already asleep.

CHAPTER TWELVE

Planning the Voyage Home

After the children's departure, there were no more running footsteps on the hardwood floors. Pachuco had no sunlit rides on the children's backs, and Veronica did not stand in front of Mirasol's cage and talk to her every morning.

Even the old man and woman seemed out of their stride.

"I sure miss Marc and Veronica's cheery voices and their huge appetites for my cooking," sighed the old woman.

The old man touched his wife's arm. "Don't worry," he told her. "They'll be back again next year. Now we'll have to get both birds out every day. They'll be missing all the attention and exercise the grandchildren gave them."

"Did you hear that, Mirasol?" said Pachuco. "They are going to let both of us out of our cages daily. We have to take advantage of this time to gain strength in our wings. We'll have to fly all over the house as fast as we can. When we take off for Pacifista we have to be in top shape."

"OK, Pachuco," agreed Mirasol, "but you had better start your diet today. Lighten up on those sunflower seeds and peanuts. And no more sweets for you."

"I know, Mirasol, you're right," said Pachuco. "Slimming down is my top priority."

When the old couple was out of earshot, Pachuco told Mirasol it was time to discuss the final plans for the voyage home.

Mirasol maneuvered her tiny body as close to Pachuco's cage as she could. She opened her black beady eyes wide. "Go ahead," she said.

"I'll start with the plans for leaving the house," said Pachuco, whispering as if the old couple could understand what he was saying. "Think about what I'm telling you, Mirasol, and let me know if there's anything that you don't think will work."

"OK, I'm listening," answered the lovebird.

Gradually the volume of the birds' exchange increased in volume until they were excitedly squawking about their plans.

"The next time the old couple goes out for the evening, I will use my beak and one talon to escape from my cage," said Pachuco. "I'm sure I've got this technique perfected. I'll just have to practice it a few times."

"How do you know you can get out of your cage?" asked Mirasol.

"I can visualize the moves that I have to make, just as if I had programmed the problem on my computer on Pacifista," said Pachuco. "It won't be difficult. You'll have to trust me on this."

"I guess I'll have to," agreed Mirasol, who cocked her head at a jaunty angle.

"Once I'm out of my cage, I'll use my beak to remove the metal pin that holds your cage closed, and free you as well," said Pachuco.

"Then what?" asked Mirasol.

"Well, you remember that the old couple will be out for the evening," Pachuco explained. "When we hear the truck coming down the street and the garage door opening, we'll be perched on top of the refrigerator."

"What will we be doing up there?" wondered Mirasol.

"That's the highest point in the kitchen," explained Pachuco. "That will be our takeoff point when the old man and woman open the door that leads to the garage. They won't be expecting us to be out of our cages, and that's the last place they'll be looking for us since it's above their eye level."

"I get it," said Mirasol. "It will be a surprise exit."

"Exactly," agreed Pachuco, "We'll take to the air at top speed and be out the garage door before it descends."

"What if we get stuck in the garage door?" asked Mirasol. Her voice was unsteady.

"We won't," said Pachuco. "There's a mechanism in the garage door that prevents it from going down when an object is entering or exiting. I heard the repairman explain this to the old man the last time he fixed the door."

"That's a relief," said Mirasol.

"We'll have to be fast," said Pachuco, "but I know we can do it!"

"I've been thinking about how we should deal with animals and birds on our journey. There are so many different types of these creatures here on Earth, I can't predict which ones we'll meet," Mirasol said. "What is important is that we stay alert and protect each other."

Just then the old man and woman came into the kitchen to let Mirasol out of her cage.

"These birds sure are shrieking this morning," said the old man. "I've never heard them continue such a lively exchange for so long. Maybe they'll be getting along better from now on."

"It will be good if they become better company for each other," said the old woman, "especially since the grandchildren have gone home."

The old man let Mirasol out of her cage, and she flew three swift loops around the house. The door leading to the long hall where the grandchildren had stayed was closed, so she could no longer go down that hall, but she flew as far as possible within the confines of the rest of the house. After three tours she came to rest on the top of the old man's head.

"Dulcita, you are full of surprises today!" exclaimed the old man. "You are making friends with Pachuco, and now you are resting on the top of my head as if it's a nest."

"I think the grandchildren had a positive effect on the birds," agreed the old woman. "I sure hope Veronica gets that lovebird for her birthday."

After an hour the old man put Mirasol back in her cage and lifted the bar from the door of Pachuco's cage. He immediately took to the air and made five circuits around the house before he gently lit on his perch in the den. He was trying to perfect his flying form.

"These birds must be having a flying competition this morning," said the old woman. "They sure are serious about getting their exercise."

"Something's going on all right," agreed the old man as he winked at Pachuco. "But this Lilac-headed Amazon isn't likely to tell us what it is."

Pachuco had rested on his perch in the den for an hour when he heard the couple talk about going to the theater that evening.

How lucky, he thought. They will be leaving the house for several hours. That is exactly the amount of time we need to finalize our plans for travel back to the wormhole and our return to Pacifista. He headed for his cage so he could tell Mirasol about this latest turn of events and discuss the plans for space travel with her.

Once in his cage, Pachuco glanced over at Mirasol. She appeared to be napping on the highest perch in her cage.

"Mirasol," squawked Pachuco. "Wake up, we leave tonight."

"What?" responded Mirasol, making an effort to open her eyes. "What did you say?"

"We are taking off tonight," said Pachuco. "The old couple is going out to a play, which will give us just enough time to escape from our cage and review our plan for space travel."

"Good grief, Pachuco, are you serious?" asked Mirasol. "I was having such a wonderful dream of my grandmother baking bread in our kitchen in Pacifista. The aroma was fantastic."

"Hopefully, you'll be back in your grandmother's kitchen before you know it," said Pachuco.

"All right, birds," said the old woman. "Keep it down, I can't concentrate on my recipe. Now, did I put two teaspoons of baking soda in the tortillas or one?"

"We'll have to talk when the couple leaves for the theater," Pachuco whispered. "We can rest for now."

After a dinner of chicken enchiladas, beans, and rice, the couple retired to their room to change for the theater. Pachuco wolfed down the dinner because he knew it would be the last New Mexican food he would ever eat. He would need his strength for the journey ahead.

Mirasol nibbled at her nuts and seeds and drank some water.

The Amazon felt more than a twinge of sadness when he saw the couple leaving for the play. He knew he would never see them again. Even though he had to return to his Kingdom in the next galaxy, they had been more than kind to him and Mirasol. He would miss them, and he was sorry that Mirasol's and his escape would cause them distress.

As soon as the truck had left the garage, he began to explain the theory of space travel through wormholes to Mirasol.

"You see, Mirasol, space travel is not an easy thing, even for technologically advanced travelers from Pacifista," he explained as he wiped his beak, sticky from enchiladas, on his lower perch.

"What makes traveling in wormholes so tough?" asked Mirasol. "Our travel from Pacifista didn't seem all that difficult."

"Wormholes bridge two universes, but there is always the danger that they will collapse into black holes, and no living thing can survive in a black hole."

"What is a black hole?" asked Mirasol, ruffling her feathers.

"A black hole is an extremely dense object in space formed by the collapse of a star," explained Pachuco. "It exerts a gravitational force so strong that nothing can escape from it."

"If what you say is true," said Mirasol, "why would we want to fool around with black holes?"

"In Pacifista when we create wormholes to visit distant galaxies, we always build a certain amount of what we call 'ghost radiation' into the system so we have a threshold of six months to return to our home planet," said Pachuco. "The 'ghost radiation' maintains the wormhole for a certain amount of time before it turns into a black hole."

"What's a threshold?" asked Mirasol, carefully preening her tail feathers.

"A threshold is a limit. We have at most six months to return to Pacifista through the wormhole in which the troll sent us here," said Pachuco. "It has been more than five months since we arrived, but returning should be no problem if we leave within the next few days."

Pachuco did not tell Mirasol all of the risks involved in travel through wormholes. They could be on the verge of collapse regardless of the threshold, or they could contain deadly asteroids. Though Pacifista scientists had developed reliable equations describing space travel, nothing was certain about a journey by wormhole.

"Astronomy and space travel sound complicated," said Mirasol.

"They can be," said Pachuco, who was working on another problem at that moment. He was maneuvering his beak and talons on the food dish in his cage. He struggled with it for twenty minutes as the metal of the food dish made a loud scraping noise against his beak.

Out of the corner of his eye Pachuco saw Mirasol looking on in silence. She sat motionless, barely breathing.

I've got to get out of this cage, thought Pachuco. Why in the world did I eat so much dinner?

Suddenly he flashed on a mental picture of his martial arts coach from Pacifista. I have to focus, he thought. He breathed deeply several times. Then he maneuvered his beak and his right talon against the sliding metal door that covered his food dish. The dish moved slightly but remained in place.

What am I doing wrong? he wondered. This plan seemed so perfect when he visualized it as if it were projected from his computer on Pacifista. Finally it came to him. He needed to use his beak and both talons, one after the other, to free up the food dish.

When he began to employ this new method, most of the food and dish landed on the linoleum floor. He took another deep breath and began pushing his body out of the space where his food dish had been. He knew the plan was a good one, but he would need to trim down his weight before he could clear the opening created when the dish fell to the floor.

Then Pachuco heard the truck approaching the house, the garage door sounded, and the old couple reappeared in the kitchen. The Amazon sheepishly backed into his cage.

"What is going on with that old truck?" asked the old woman crossly. "I've been telling you to take it in to the garage for weeks. Now we've missed the play."

"Never mind," said the old man. "They'll put the play on again next season, and I'll be sure to get tickets. I'll take the truck in for repairs tomorrow."

The old woman caught sight of the food on the floor below Pachuco's cage. "What is this?" she asked, glaring at Pachuco.

Pachuco hung his head.

"Since when do you throw your dish and perfectly good food on the floor?" asked the old man. "We will be giving you far less food in the future if you keep this up."

Pachuco knew that the deadline for return to Pacifista by wormhole was only days away. He would have to settle for seeds and water until he and Mirasol escaped from the house.

Five days passed before the old couple went out again in the evening. This time they emptied Pachuco's food container before leaving as a precaution.

"We're not coming home to another of your messes," said the old man as the couple left by the garage door.

Pachuco was sure he could manipulate his beak and talons to eject the food container. He had just begun to focus on the motion of his talons.

Mirasol cried, "Be careful, Pachuco, I hear the old couple's truck coming down the street. It's heading for the garage!"

She was right. She had picked up the sound of the truck when Pachuco, intent on exiting his cage, had not.

"Thanks for the heads up, Mirasol," said Pachuco as he shifted his food dish back to its original position. "Escaping from my cage is more difficult than I would have thought. I wonder what happened to the old couple this time."

The old man and woman came into the kitchen in a huff.

"There are our computer movie tickets, right here on the table! Why did you forget them?" asked the old man. "Now it's too late to go to the show."

"I put them on the table so you could pick them up on your way out the door the way you usually do," said the old woman. "Let's cover the birds and go to bed."

It was another week before the couple left on a social engagement in the evening.

"Tonight has got to be it," Pachuco told Mirasol. "We have only a few days to reach the wormhole and return to Pacifista before the wormhole collapses in on itself and becomes a black hole. Do you remember the details of our plan for leaving the house?" he asked.

"Yes, all of them," she answered. "Go on, Pachuco, get out of your cage before the old couple returns again."

Pachuco dumped his food dish on the floor with his beak and talons. Then he shoved his head, talons, and body out of the opening that until several seconds before had held his food dish. It was an extremely tight fit, and at first he didn't think he would make it out of the cage. He pushed and pushed, and finally with a burst of energy and a firm thrust from his wings and body, he exited the cage.

Mirasol was jumping up and down on her lowest perch.

"You did it! You did it!" she exclaimed. "I never thought you'd make it out of your cage."

Pachuco took three victory laps around the house. "I knew I could do it, Mirasol," he shrieked.

"Pachuco, free me from me cage," insisted Mirasol. "We don't have time for you to fly aimlessly around the house."

Then he approached her cage, and attempted to lift the metal bar that fastened the opening of her cage. He tried several times to lift the bar, but it was stuck. His beak was too large to fit on the loop in the bar.

"I don't know about this, Mirasol," he said. "We are going to have to work together to open your cage. You will have to exit your cage the same way I did. I will help you by lifting up the metal device that covers your seed tray."

"OK," said Mirasol. "I'll count to three. You lift and I'll push myself out. One, two, three."

The two birds concentrated on their effort, and before Mirasol had said three she was out of the cage and propelled onto the floor. Her dish fell before she did, scattering seeds all over the floor.

"Are you all right?" asked Pachuco, who had never seen her on the floor in all the time he had known her as a lovebird.

"I'm fine," said Mirasol, who quickly flew to the top of her cage. "I exerted too much force in trying to eject myself from the cage."

"Let's go up to the top of the refrigerator and wait for the old couple to come home," said Pachuco. "They should be here soon."

The birds flew up to the top of the refrigerator. Pachuco whistled from his perch there as it was his habit to whistle from locations he was not supposed to frequent, and the top of the refrigerator was one of them. Mirasol nodded off. They had no idea how long they would have to wait for the old couple.

An hour later they heard the old man's truck gasping and sputtering as it approached the house. Mirasol awoke with a start. The garage door creaked as it opened.

Minutes later the back door cracked open as the old couple climbed the two steps that led from the garage into the kitchen.

Mirsol whispered to Pachuco, "One, two, three, go!"

The birds flew over the couple's heads and under the garage door that came to an immediate halt in its descent. The old couple seemed to have no idea the birds were escaping from the house.

In seconds the birds were flying free.

Pachuco and Mirasol escaped into the night sky, flying higher and higher and closer and closer to the stars.

CHAPTER THIRTEEN

The Birds Head for the Wormhole

T he first night of flight was the longest Pachuco had ever known. He sensed large birds and animals scurrying close to him and sounding off in the darkness.

His experience with animals and birds in the wild was limited. From the windows of the old couple's house he had once seen a tall, speckled bird that the old woman had identified as a roadrunner, and she had named the tiny, hovering birds that gathered at the feeder on the porch as hummingbirds. He remembered having seen two cats in the yard, a sleek Siamese, and the other a bushy, long-haired variety.

None of these animal sightings prepared him for his first night abroad. He was weary and afraid and could not help thinking that maybe he and Mirasol should have stayed in the old couple's kitchen. He could not believe it, but he felt helpless without the protective bars on his cage.

Mirasol seemed to have no second thoughts about their escape from the house and was gliding easily, high in the air. With great effort, Pachuco caught up with her and asked her if she was certain that they were flying away from the mountains and towards the river as they had planned.

They were returning to the great river near the location where Mirasol had nested with the sparrows. It was there Pachuco believed they would discover the wormhole, high above the river basin.

His astronomy teacher had taught him that wormholes were concentrated above bodies of water, gaining energy from the flowing and gushing watercourses and the currents that often accompanied them.

"Yes, I'm sure of it," she answered, "though it might be a good idea for us to head for a cottonwood tree and get a few winks of sleep."

Pachuco agreed. Strangely, he felt drowsy in spite of the adrenaline pumping in his veins.

"You choose the tree, Mirasol," he said.

Mirasol flew to a fifty-foot cottonwood and made for the highest branches of the deciduous poplar. Its crown had large, widely spreading branches.

"We should be safe up here," said the lovebird, surveying the night sky. "Hopefully not too many predators make it up this high."

Mirasol fell asleep quickly. Pachuco balanced on a branch on his talons and listened to the orchestra of night sounds. He could not identify the birds and animals making these sounds, and that inability to distinguish the source of the shrieks and rustlings made them all the more terrifying.

He was used to sleeping in the secure kitchen of the old couple's house. The loudest noise in the kitchen was from a movie or television show the couple was watching in the nearby den or firecrackers outside on the Fourth of July.

He thought about the old couple. How had they reacted when they realized the birdcages were empty, and he and Mirasol had escaped into the night? He could picture the shock and horror on their faces. The old woman might have sat down at the worn kitchen table and cried. The old man probably shook his head in disbelief more than once.

Pachuco had a mental picture of the old man telling the old woman, "Didn't I tell you? I knew something was up with those birds!"

In his mind's eye, Pachuco could see the old man getting up early in the morning to scour the neighborhood in his truck to see if he could spot his missing birds. Little did the old man know that by then we would be miles away from the house on our way to the great river, thought the Amazon.

Mirasol awakened Pachuco at dawn. "Get up, Pachuco," she said. "The river is far away, and we'll be thirsty long before we arrive there."

Mirasol flew off her perch into the cloudless New Mexican sky. Pachuco followed her, squawking. He was not used to exercise this early in the morning, especially without his breakfast of sliced fruits, vegetables, and scrambled egg.

Surely I can do without food for a few days, he thought. He looked over at Mirasol; she didn't seem to be bothered by the lack of food.

The lovebird and the Amazon flew in tandem toward the river. Soon Pachuco was winded. He came to rest on a log near a wooded area with a stream, home to a family of mallard ducks.

"Pachuco, get off the ground," Mirasol shrieked. "That is the most dangerous place to light."

Before Pachuco could lift off into the air, he felt the presence of an animal creeping forward, slyly approaching him from the rear.

From the corner of his eye, Pachuco could see a brown and black dog-like creature with large erect ears, a wet, black nose, unblinking yellow eyes, and a downward turning tail. The animal had long legs in proportion to his slim body.

Pachuco's first thoughts were of Diamante, his black Labrador.

"This is a dog, just like Diamante," he reassured Mirasol, who was wildly pacing on a nearby branch. "Look how trusty his eyes are."

"This is not a domesticated dog, Pachuco," she squawked. "Get out of there now!"

Mirasol dive-bombed the creature as he was about to stealthily charge at Pachuco. She bit him deeply several times on his flank with her sharp beak as he was about to leap into the air. He howled with pain, throwing her ten feet into the air, but he gave up his intention to snap up the Amazon with his toothy jaws.

Pachuco was terrified as he managed to take to the air. He and Mirasol resumed their flight in a westward direction.

"Never forget," said Mirasol, as she led Pachuco in flight, "do not go down to the ground. If you need to rest, light on a tree branch. This is the wild. You may see animals that remind you of Diamante, but believe me, they are not friendly. They all want to devour you."

"You're right, Mirasol," said Pachuco. "I'll take nothing for granted when it comes to animals in the wild."

Mirasol and Pachuco continued their journey. They came upon a golf course with a large pond. As it was still early, few golfers were about. Pachuco asked Mirasol if he might get a drink of water from the pond.

She studied the terrain carefully and said, "All right, Pachuco, have your drink, but be quick about it. I'll be watching."

Pachuco lighted at the pond's edge and began to drink. He was exceedingly thirsty from the morning of flying. Before he could satisfy his thirst, a fifty-inch-long bird with a seven-foot wingspan landed gracefully next to him in the pond's shallow water. The bird was blue-gray with whitish under parts and black streaks on its belly. Its head was white with a black stripe above the eyes that continued into plumes behind its head. Its legs, neck, and blade-like bill were all extremely long.

Again, Mirasol spotted the threat before Pachuco did and dove down to strike the massive predator.

But this time she could not contain the bird. Instead, the huge beast grabbed Mirasol, tossed her into the air with its massive beak as if she were weightless, and swallowed her whole. All the while it squawked a deafening "Frawnk! Frawnk!"

Pachuco looked up just as the giant blue bird gulped Mirasol down. She became a lump in the bird's thin, crooked neck.

Pachuco bristled; he was in frenzy.

"Mirasol, tell me this is not happening!" he roared.

Pachuco plunged his hooked beak into the massive bird's neck just below the bulge that was Mirasol. He bit the bird over and over, trying to balance his body on the gigantic bird's neck.

The Amazon was relentless and almost exhausted when the mammoth bird made another guttural sound, gagged, and disgorged the distressed and startled lovebird.

"Gosh, Mirasol, are you all right?" shrieked Pachuco. "I never thought I'd see you again!"

Mirasol took several deep breaths. She seemed unable to speak, and her feathers were rumpled and wet from her encounter with the great bird.

"I'm not sure I can fly until my feathers dry out," she said when she was able to speak. "I don't think I have any broken bones."

Hearing this, Pachuco continued squawking and fanned out his feathers in full display, hoping to intimidate the huge bird that continued to threaten Mirasol.

After several minutes, Mirasol said, "I can fly now, Pachuco. I'm just winded. Let's stop and rest when we see the next wooded area."

Pachuco and Mirasol took a half hour break when they reached the next group of trees. Mirasol preened the feathers on her entire body.

"We are getting close to the river basin," announced the lovebird. "There are many more birds of prey by the river, so we have to be especially careful."

"You're right, Mirasol," agreed Pachuco, who had been inspecting the lovebird's body carefully. "Are you sure that's not a scratch on your talon?"

"No," said Mirasol. "I was just dazed. The rest has done me good."

"What was it like being swallowed by the great bird?" asked Pachuco.

"It was incredibly terrifying," answered Mirasol shuddering. "I really don't want to talk about it."

The birds flew on. Shortly afterwards they reached the river which was not deep but was teeming with wildlife, as Mirasol had predicted. The sight of the water seemed to remind the lovebird that she was unbearably thirsty after her encounter with the great bird.

Without taking time to cautiously inspect her surroundings as was her usual practice, she dove into the shallow water at the river's edge. Splashing her small body in the cool water, she suddenly heard the piercing "kree-eee-ar," that could only be the call of another large bird of prey.

This predator had a four-foot wingspan, a rust-red tail, and pale, striped breast feathers. The bird measured a full twenty-five inches in length, and the ends of its wings were black.

Pachuco could see the bird's piercing eyes that had turned their sights on tiny Mirasol.

Not again, he thought. He understood now that though Mirasol was shrewd and tough, she was such a tiny bird that she was a natural target for birds of prey.

"Watch out, Mirasol!" shrieked Pachuco. He tried to warn her, but it was too late.

The red-tailed bird swooped down and took off with Mirasol firmly in its talons.

Pachuco trembled when he saw the ferocity of the bird's curved bill and yellow talons.

Mirasol was paralyzed by the predator's talons. Her small eyes flashed, and Pachuco was not sure if she were breathing.

Seconds after the predator seized Mirasol, Pachuco swung into action.

"Oh, no you don't," he squawked to the red-tail, not caring whether the bird could understand him or not.

"Hang on, Mirasol. I'm on my way," he sang out.

He mustered all his strength and flew up towards the huge predator. The Amazon attacked the red-tail on its talons with his hooked beak until dark clumps of the red-tail's blood trickled towards the Earth.

The red-tail clutched fiercely at Mirasol's small body as Pachuco aggressively attacked. Finally the spotted bird reluctantly released

Mirasol, letting out another resounding "kree-eee-ar" as Mirasol made a wobbly ascent skyward.

"Take off, Mirasol," Pachuco shouted, "I'll catch up with you."

Mirasol was able to dart off at moderate speed, leaving Pachuco and the red-tail behind. Pachuco lit into the wounded predator, attacking wherever he could find an opening. More of the red-tail's dark blood spilled onto the dusty riverbank.

The red-tail appeared to have been ready for an easy prey and was not prepared for the viciousness of Pachuco's assault. He hovered in place with Pachuco hanging on in mid-air with his beak digging into the predator's breast, trying to avoid the red-tail's beak and talons.

Feathers of parrot and red-tail flew wildly. At last the red-tail seemed convinced Pachuco was not giving up and with a powerful thrust shook the Amazon off his body. The red-tail sailed upward. Pachuco looked after his opponent and imagined that the red-tail was rising on columns of hot air that would carry him to aerial lookouts on the high mesa to seek out easier prey.

When Pachuco saw three of the predator's tail feathers floating in slow motion down to Earth, he remembered that he had learned in class at the Palace on Pacifista that feathers, especially red tail feathers, were considered sacred to many native tribes.

He decided to gather up the feathers in his beak to transport them through the wormhole. Once back in Pacifista he would present them to the troll in hopes of breaking Malvado's evil spell.

Pachuco flew on high in the sky with the red tail feathers in his beak. He was still moving in a westerly direction when he faintly heard Mirasol's cry.

"Mirasol, is that you?" he asked breathlessly as he attempted to speak as he held onto the tail feathers, not an easy task.

"Yes, Pachuco," she said weakly.

"Are you hurt?" he asked, again examining her for injuries when he had her in view. He noticed a scratch running down her back.

"It's nothing serious," she said. "I'll be as good as new in a few days. What about you? Lean down. I think I see a mean cut on your head."

"It probably looks worse than it is," said Pachuco. "It doesn't bother me."

"You saved me from the clutches of two predators," said Mirasol. "I owe you my life."

"And you saved me from the wild dog," said Pachuco. "He would have snapped me up if you hadn't come to the rescue."

"We are working well together," said Mirasol. "I don't think we would make it alone in the wilds of Planet Earth."

"We should almost be in the vicinity of the wormhole," announced Pachuco. "We'll tackle that tomorrow. I think we both need to rest now. It's been an exhausting day."

"Let's find another cottonwood tree and head up to the top branches for the night," Mirasol said.

"Sounds good," said Pachuco. He was grateful he and Mirasol had survived the day and prayed that tomorrow's travel through the wormhole would be as successful.

When they reached branches in the crown of an eighty-foot cottonwood, both birds nodded off almost immediately.

Pachuco began to snore and then slept. He dreamed of a huge meal of Mexican, New Mexican, and American dishes.

He was in the kitchen in the old couple's house. The table was heaped with plates full of enchiladas, rice, pinto beans, tortillas, *birria, carne asada, posole, menudo, barbacoa, pollo en mole, carnitas, chile verde*, and *lengua*. And, of course, there was an extra large pizza with an assortment of toppings.

For dessert there were pastel de chocolate tres leches, vanilla ice cream, caramel apples, and cherry, apple, and pumpkin pies.

He could smell the rich aroma of the combination of all the foods heating on the stovetop and baking in the oven.

And Marc and Veronica were sitting around the table with the old couple sharing in the feast and filling and refilling his food dish with more and more food.

He was full though his stomach was emptier than it had ever been in his life on Pacifista or on Earth.

The sounds of the forest did not penetrate this dream.

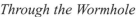

CHAPTER FOURTEEN

Through the Wormhole

Mirasol woke at dawn, as was her custom in the outdoors. The cut on her back from the red-tail's talons was painful, but when she turned her neck to see it, it was no longer bleeding and seemed to be on the mend.

"Pachuco, wake up!" she called, looking over to the Lilac-headed Amazon who was still immobile on the perch next to her.

"Where are we?" asked Pachuco groggily. He shook his entire body.

"We're in the basin of the great river," said Mirasol. "And you'd better wake up if we're going to make it anywhere close to that wormhole today."

"You've got that right, Mirasol," he said.

Mirasol gazed up at Pachuco as he preened. She could barely detect a thin red scar on his head.

"The cut on your head seems to be healing well," she told Pachuco.

"The wound on your back looks better, too, though it seems larger than I realized yesterday," said Pachuco. "Gosh, Mirasol, I can't believe that you managed to fly so well with that wound."

"Flying is like breathing to me," said Mirasol. "Nothing can prevent me from flying."

"That's the truth," said Pachuco. "Are you hungry this morning? Should we hunt up some worms or grubs for breakfast?"

"I am not hungry in the least," said Mirasol. "Do you think you can attempt space travel on an empty stomach?"

"Yes, I'll be fine," said Pachuco. "I had the most amazing dream last night of a feast in the old couple's kitchen. The old man and women were there and so were Veronica and Marc. I ate so much that the meal will last me for days."

"You're not hungry today because you dreamed of food last night?" asked Mirasol. She doubted this was possible, but she had always found Pachuco to be truthful. Maybe this was some new twist on animal psychology she had never studied on Pacifista.

When Pachuco had sufficiently preened his feathers, he turned to Mirasol. "Now I have to tell you more details of wormhole travel."

Mirasol was floored. "More details? I thought you'd told me all the details."

"Well, not quite," admitted Pachuco. "While we are perched in this cottonwood tree, this is a great opportunity for us to practice meditation. We will need to be deep in meditation when we travel through the wormhole."

"What are you talking about? I don't know a thing about meditation," said Mirasol. "Why didn't you tell me about this before?"

"I guess it slipped my mind," said Pachuco. "But it's not a difficult skill to master," explained Pachuco. "It's even enjoyable."

"Why in the world would I want to learn to meditate just as we are about to go off on a voyage through space and time?" asked Mirasol as she cocked her tiny head.

"When you meditate, you create a capsule of positive energy around your entire body that will protect you from negative elements that we may encounter in space," said Pachuco.

"What kinds of negative elements?" asked Mirasol, coming to realize that Pachuco had been holding out on her about some of the dangers of space travel.

"Well, ghost radiation needs to be added to the wormhole to keep it from collapsing. This type of radiation can be harmful to living creatures if they are not sheltered by a capsule of positive energy."

Mirasol shook her head. "What do we have to do to create this capsule?"

She was beginning to worry that meditation was going to be a skill that she would not be able to master before they entered the wormhole.

"Meditation is simple," said Pachuco. "I learned it from my martial arts teacher on Pacifista, and he was an expert. We will practice it here for half an hour and then for another half an hour before we enter the wormhole."

Pachuco carefully gave her the instructions his teacher had given him. "You sit silently in a safe and comfortable place and take several deep breaths," he said, drawing his breath in and out three times. "Then you close your eyes and focus on a particular thought, word, or your breath."

"That sounds easy enough," said Mirasol. "What's the catch?"

"There's no catch," said Pachuco. "You might want to watch your breath or picture Pacifista, our destination at the end of the wormhole."

"I guess I can do that," said Mirasol. "It doesn't sound too difficult."

"It's not," said Pachuco. "It's important if stray thoughts creep into your mind, don't make an effort to get rid of them. Just return and focus on the subject of your meditation."

"OK, I'm ready to give it a go," said Mirasol.

"Remember to close your eyes and focus," instructed Pachuco.

The two birds balanced on the top branch in the umbrella of the cottonwood tree. They closed their eyes and took deep breaths. Mirasol opened one eye and could see Pachuco almost immediately go into a deep trance.

This is incredible, she thought. It will take me hours to become that focused and relaxed at the same time. Then it occurred to her, it's *impossible* to be focused and relaxed at the same moment!

"Pachuco, this is absurd!" Mirasol squeaked.

"Mirasol, simmer down," said Pachuco as if he were awakened suddenly from a deep sleep. "Did I forget to tell you not to talk when you meditate? Now concentrate and give it a try."

Mirasol closed her eyes and tried to focus. But when she closed her eyes images of the wild dog and the two immense birds came into view, and she was not able to concentrate.

"I know I'm not supposed to talk," said Mirasol, "but I just can't focus!"

"Sure you can," said Pachuco. "Don't try too hard. Let your mind go."

Mirasol forgot her reservations and closed her eyes. She breathed deeply several times. Then she focused on her home in Pacifista. She saw her grandmother, her castle, and the forests where she had hiked and studied nature. Her mind wandered more than it focused on one image, but gradually she concentrated on the forest with the great waterfall cascading into a pool below.

She smiled when she recognized the waterfall. She followed Pachuco's instructions, and when her mind drifted she returned again to the mental picture of the waterfall.

After a half hour Pachuco called to Mirasol and told her the first meditation session was over.

"It seemed to drag on for hours, Pachuco," said Mirasol.

"It will get easier," said Pachuco. "Let's take off."

The two ascended high over the great river. At first water fowl followed them, but after a while they flew on alone. Mirasol flew first, gliding and gaining altitude. She saw Pachuco following, glancing continually in all directions to spot the wormhole.

When they were high above the clouds in the thinning atmosphere, Pachuco called out to Mirasol. "The wormhole should be close. Let's do our final meditation."

"How can we meditate without a branch to sit on?" asked Mirasol.

"We'll just have to make do," said Pachuco. "Pretend you are treading water in a stream in Pacifista."

The pair began meditating.

"This is more difficult than meditating while perched on a tree branch," said Mirasol. "I don't think I can do it."

"Focus and concentrate like you did before," said Pachuco. "I know you can."

Mirasol opened one eye and peeked at Pachuco, who again seemed to be in a deep sleep. She squirmed uneasily as she strove to flap her wings and concentrate at the same time.

When the session was over, Pachuco told Mirasol, "The wormhole is just about a quarter mile above us from my latest calculations. Let's fly directly upward."

The two lifted off and soared upward, but the wormhole was nowhere to be seen.

"I wonder where it could be," said Pachuco. "My calculations are always precise."

"I have a feeling it's an eighth of a mile to the south," said Mirasol.

"What makes you think so?" asked Pachuco.

"I don't know," said Mirasol. "It's just a hunch."

"OK, let's give it a try," said Pachuco. "I've learned to rely on your intuition."

After flying an eighth-mile southward they came upon an enormous, gyrating, worm-shaped structure. The wormhole emitted deafening, low-pitched, jarring sounds. It was streaked with red, yellow, and black markings that meandered up and down its expanse.

"Don't tell me we are going to travel in that?" Mirasol said, horrified. "My stomach is already lurching."

"Yes, we are," said Pachuco. "If your stomach is bothering you, start your meditation. That should help."

"I thought you said that we would find the energy marker so we would know this wormhole was the one that brought us here from Pacifista," said Mirasol.

"That's our first task," agreed Pachuco. Mirasol could see him gingerly flying into the wide bottom of the wormhole. He gave Mirasol the red-tail feathers to hold in her beak while he investigated.

She began to work on her meditation while he searched for the energy marker.

"I found it, Mirasol," he called when he emerged from the wormhole several minutes later carrying a spray of roseweed, a bright purple flower native to Pacifista.

"I know that plant well," said Mirasol. "I've sketched roseweed many times on my hikes in Pacifista."

Pachuco took the red-tail feathers back from Mirasol.

"Is it time to start traveling up the wormhole, then?" asked Mirasol as her whole body shook with apprehension.

"Yes," said Pachuco. "Give me the three red-tail feathers and begin working your way up the wormhole. The apparatus makes a grating racket, but try not to focus on it. Remember to close your eyes and meditate. Do not look back. Fly like the wind, Mirasol, and don't think about me. Do you promise?"

"Y-Y-Yes," said Mirasol. She wondered how he could make her agree to such a thing. He had saved her twice from wild creatures, and she knew that if he were in danger she would do what she could to rescue him. She had, after all, rescued him from the wild dog. They were a team.

But she promised because she did not want to delay their journey. Pachuco had made it clear that they had only hours before their window to return to Pacifista would be closing.

"OK, Mirasol, start meditating and climb into the wormhole. Don't stop ascending until you see the light in the forests of Pacifista," said Pachuco.

The two were speechless. They had had so many adventures together. The last two days alone had seemed to last for years.

"Pachuco, if we don't meet again . . . ." Mirasol began. Her eyes filled with tears.

"Don't go there, Mirasol," Pachuco raised a wing to stop her. "I'll see you soon in Pacifista.

Just as Mirasol disappeared into the spinning tornado of the wormhole, she screamed, "Pachuco, you must have dropped the red-tail feathers!"

"Go on up the wormhole," instructed Pachuco. "I will find the tail feathers. No arguments now." He glanced downwards and saw the feathers fluttering slowly through cloud cover towards Earth.

"I must have those feathers!" he screeched and dove down toward them. "We will never overcome Malvado without them."

As soon as he reached the feathers and recaptured them, he flew upwards at top speed and followed Mirasol up the wormhole.

Mirasol was nowhere to be seen. She had begun her journey slowly but her speed soon accelerated. She wondered if her speed exceeded the speed of light. Travel at such a great velocity seemed impossible to grasp. As she proceeded up the wormhole, it narrowed from its broad base to a slimmer and more compact structure. She felt the wormhole catapulting her upward as if thrust by a giant slingshot. The intensity of the wormhole's raucous rasping did not abate.

Was Pachuco flying somewhere behind? She thought she heard him enter the wormhole, but she was so far ahead of him that she could not be sure. She tried to meditate and listen for his progress below at the same time. It was not possible.

"Pachuco, Pachuco, are you there?" she cried as loudly as she could, but her tiny voice was lost in the roar from the wormhole.

He did not answer. Only the wormhole with its thunderous bellowing offered an answer. And it was not the one she wanted.

Then everything went black.

• • •

Mirasol woke with a start hours later. The roar of the wormhole had not subsided, and she still could not determine if Pachuco were following behind her in his energy capsule. She saw a streak of greenish-white light directly in front of her. It appeared that she was reaching the far side of the wormhole, which was as broad as the near side had been.

Mirasol was excited. Where am I? she wondered.

No matter how loudly she called out to Pachuco, he did not respond. She had to believe he was floating below, deep in a trance of meditation. If only it were so!

Finally the brilliant light reaching her eyes convinced her that she could fly out of the wormhole and make for solid ground. After the avalanche of sound that was the wormhole, the relative silence of the land was deafening.

Then she saw them, the spires of Pachuco's Palace and her castle as well. I am home, she thought. She sighed deeply. I am truly back to everything I hold dear.

She had almost forgotten that Pachuco had told her to fly as far away from the wormhole as she could as soon as she reached Pacifista. She flew rapidly and lighted on the spire of Pachuco's Palace. Just as she wrapped her talons around the narrow spire, she heard an enormous explosion and felt the earth move as if there had been an earthquake. The spire moved back and forth as if it were a spirited metronome.

How could Pachuco have survived such an impact, she wondered. Surely, he had not. She remained glued to the spire for an hour, watching in the direction of the wormhole.

Then, suddenly a bird as black and shiny as a crow came into view. Something about the bird's shape was familiar.

"Pachuco, is that you?" she shrieked.

"Mirasol, we made it!" exclaimed Pachuco, wiping dust out of his eyes with his talons. "We're home. We've made it back to Pacifista."

"I'm thrilled to see you, Pachuco! *We have survived!* And the wormhole, is it gone?" asked Mirasol.

"Yes, it collapsed in on itself," said Pachuco. "No one will be traveling though it again. We got out just in time."

"What happened to your green feathers and lilac head?" asked Mirasol. She wondered if there were such a thing as a black parrot.

"They're still there, I hope," said Pachuco, "under layers of dust and debris from the wormhole. I still have the red-tail feathers, too."

Mirasol proposed that they take off for the Pacifista Nature Preserve to clean up. They both needed to wash in the Preserve's pond and to eat grain from a field nearby planted for migratory birds.

The birds reached the Nature Preserve just as the sun was setting. Mirasol splashed joyfully in the warm water of the pond while Pachuco dunked himself fifteen times to remove all the soot and debris from the wormhole. Then he shook out his feathers, which were back to their green and lilac colors once more, and dried them in what was left of the afternoon sunlight.

The birds ate as much of the grain in the field as they could hold. Pachuco was so famished that he did not even complain about the lackluster food.

Then the sun began to set. The birds had almost forgotten the kaleidoscoping rainbows on Pacifista.

"Look, Pachuco," shouted Mirasol. "The rainbows are still shifting into ever more magnificent shades every few seconds."

Pachuco appeared exhausted from his ordeal, but he squawked as he took in the stunning display. "Mirasol, we've made it home."

"Yes, we have," said Mirasol. "Maybe tomorrow we can look in on our families."

"I wonder if Diamante will recognize me as an Amazon parrot," Pachuco said with a yawn.

"We'll see, Pachuco," said Mirasol, who did not believe a black Labrador retriever and an Amazon parrot would get along. "It's time to seek out a high tree branch and get some sleep."

The two birds flew up to the highest branch of a tall elm. They fell into a deep sleep almost as they lighted.

For once, Pachuco did not snore.

CHAPTER FIFTEEN

The Birds Visit Home

The birds awoke at dawn the next morning. Pachuco was thrilled to be back in Pacifista and eager to explore his Kingdom and become reacquainted with his family. He had a huge appetite and was ready to graze at the wheat field for migratory birds in the Nature Preserve where they had slept.

"Are you hungry, Mirasol?" he asked when they had finished preening.

"Yes, I am," she answered with enthusiasm. "Let's go down to the wheat field."

Pachuco was surprised at her response. He had never seen her so interested in food. It appeared that they both needed sustenance to make up for the meals they had missed traveling to and through the wormhole.

They plummeted down to the wheat field from the high elm branch, leaving the red-tail feathers in the protected area where they had slept.

"Shouldn't we take the feathers with us?" asked Mirasol.

"No," answered Pachuco. "They will just be in the way while we're eating."

They landed in the wheat field and began to forage once again on the abundant grain.

Suddenly Pachuco took a sharp breath. He sensed something stirring next to him. From his peripheral vision he saw a figure the size of a child. Pachuco's eyes dilated and his feathers ruffled.

Malvado!

Mirasol sighted the troll and choked on the wheat in her beak.

"So you two are back!" squealed the troll. "One of my guards said they spotted you yesterday. I told them it was impossible for you to have returned to Pacifista, but here you are."

"Mirasol," Pachuco whispered, "Fly up to the elm branch where we spent the night, and bring back the red-tail feathers. Then gather a few branches of mistletoe." Pachuco knew that from Mirasol's study of biology she could easily identify mistletoe, the plant his father had told him would thwart the troll's evil powers.

"B-B-But I can't leave you here with him," Mirasol gasped.

"I'll be OK, Mirasol," said Pachuco. "I need those feathers and the mistletoe! And when you return, light in the branches of the nearby spruce tree and call out three times as loudly as you can. Now take off."

Mirasol ascended into the air and was gone. The troll stared blankly after her for several seconds, as if he could not fathom her swift departure.

Pachuco studied the wizened creature and decided his appearance, if nothing else, was dramatically changed. He was still only as tall as a six-year-old child, but his clothing was much more sophisticated than it had been the last time Pachuco had seen him. He wore a tiny velvet cape, purple leather breeches, and purple shoes that seemed to fit his broad feet comfortably. His long white beard was skillfully trimmed. Pachuco looked instinctively for the spider tattoo on the top of the troll's right hand and quickly spotted it.

Malvado had been studying him as well. This gave Pachuco time to recognize Malvado's cape. He was certain it had been cut down from one of his own. His feathers bristled.

"How dare you wear my royal cape, Malvado?" shrieked Pachuco.

"I wear your cape because I am the King of Pacifista, or have you forgotten?" asked Malvado in his high-pitched voice. He seemed to have no trouble understanding Pachuco's language.

"You were never much of a King when you were human, and surely you have not returned to reclaim your Kingdom as a Lilac-headed Amazon parrot," said the troll who rolled his eyes and let out a roar of laughter.

"Malvado, you are a thief," said Pachuco. "You have stolen the throne of the Kingdom of Pacifista for the second time. You have no right to rule here."

"No? And who is going to stop me? An Amazon parrot and a peach-throated lovebird? I think I will be in power for a long time," said Malvado, throwing back his head and cackling. "I'm sure you will be interested in the changes I have made in the government of Pacifista."

Pachuco came as close to a snarl as a parrot could get. "What changes?" he asked. Pachuco had no desire to listen to the troll's drivel, but he had to stall to give Mirasol time to return with the feathers and mistletoe.

"Your mother, the former Queen, is confined to the servant's quarters of the Royal Palace. She has only one servant. Out of my immense generosity, I allow her to entertain her former subjects once a week. I do this so the citizens of Pacifista can see what a kind-hearted ruler I am."

"Don't make me laugh," shrieked Pachuco. "You don't have a kind or generous bone in your body."

"How are you preventing her from leaving the Palace?" asked Pachuco.

"I have put armed guards by the doors of her rooms. If she wants to stay alive, she must abide by my rules," said the troll.

Pachuco knew his mother would never endure such treatment unless she had no choice. He shook with rage.

"And that's far from all," said Malvado who seemed delighted by Pachuco's reaction.

"I am now charging all my subjects a sixty percent tax on all their property. This tax, in addition to the income tax already in place, goes directly into the royal treasury for the upkeep of my family," said the troll.

"The citizens of Pacifista must be starving under your rule," squawked Pachuco.

"What's more," continued Malvado, "we have no more useless health clinics, libraries, or child or elder care. These programs are wasteful as they put no money in the coffers of my Kingdom."

"Malvado, you are the essence of evil," said Pachuco, who knew that trying to reason with the troll was useless, but he had to continue stalling until Mirasol appeared. "I can't believe you have made all these changes in so little time. You have destroyed the foundation of Pacifista society that my father and grandfather worked so hard to build."

Malvado laughed again. His laugh seemed to pour out of his throat.

"You sound like you think you're in a position to stop me, green bird," he said. "I told you before that you have no authority here, and this time I mean to make you believe it!"

Pachuco heard Mirasol squawking three times from the branch of the spruce tree.

She's back just in time, he thought. He had been afraid he would not be able to ward off an attack from Malvado without the feathers and mistletoe branches. Pachuco thought it odd that Malvado appeared without guards. He also found it peculiar that Malvado had assumed the form of a troll rather than transforming into a giant, a much more threatening figure. The troll must have thought an Amazon and a lovebird to be adversaries he could easily overcome.

"Listen, Malvado," said Pachuco in as calm a voice as he could muster, "in New Mexico, a state in the United States on Planet Earth, where you sent us as eggs through the wormhole, there is an Indian tribe called the Mescalero Apaches."

"So what of it?" asked Malvado. "They cannot protect you here. You and that lovebird friend of yours are going to die right here on Pacifista."

"The Mescalero Apaches believe that the red-tailed birds represent awareness," said Pachuco. "The red-tail is a messenger and can move between the seen and unseen world. We met one of these birds on earth and had the fight of our lives for survival."

"Do I care?" squeaked Malvado in his falsetto. "Hogwash from Indian tribes on an under-technologically developed planet in the next galaxy means nothing to me. Don't waste my time."

Pachuco raised his wing to signal Mirasol to bring him the red-tail feathers and mistletoe. As she placed them in his beak he pronounced in a brash and piercing voice that echoed throughout the Nature Preserve, "Behold these vibrant feathers and evergreen branches, symbols of spirit, wisdom, and power."

Malvado seemed mesmerized by the feathers and branches. His eyes were glued to them as if he were becoming hypnotized.

"These feathers are the gift of the red-tail. They can and will destroy all evil-doers," pronounced Pachuco screaming as loudly as his lungs allowed. "The mistletoe also overcomes evildoers."

Mirasol added her small voice to the din, shrieking, "You are wicked, Malvado! You will not be victorious."

The two continued their chanting for a half hour. Malvado seemed to be able to do nothing but sit cross-eyed, eyes glazed, staring at the red-tail feathers and mistletoe branches. The birds had just about exhausted their voices when the field lurched suddenly, sending them tumbling. Mirasol flew up into the trees but Pachuco was swept forcefully against a log. He remembered Mirasol's advice to stay away from the ground, but his wing was pinned in place by the massive piece of wood. He was unable to move.

A purple cloud settled over the forest and moved into the wheat field. It was a thick fog, and Pachuco feared that Malvado was going to attack him and Mirasol through the impenetrable mist.

After several minutes the fog cleared, and Mirasol flew down from her perch to help Pachuco free his wing from the log. Mirasol struggled with the log, but was unable to budge it.

When she had expended all her energy, Pachuco told her to fly up to the trees in case Malvado was lurking close by.

"Never," said Mirasol, making a final strenuous effort with her beak that freed Pachuco.

Then they both flew up to a tree branch and stared down into the wheat field.

"Mirasol, have you seen the troll?" asked Pachuco.

"No," said Mirasol. "He's nowhere to be seen."

"Do you think the red-tail feathers and mistletoe have destroyed him?" Pachuco asked."

"Wouldn't it be wonderful if they did?" asked Mirasol. "Those Mescalero Apaches had strong medicine if it works here on Pacifista."

"And my father's prediction about the powers of the mistletoe has proven true as well," said Pachuco.

Pachuco looked down and noticed a swirling tail of energy like a comet giving off a mournful, moaning sound they could easily identify as Malvado's high-pitched voice. The comet became smaller and smaller and eventually disappeared from view.

"The red-tail feathers worked! The tail feathers worked!" exclaimed Pachuco. "That is the last we'll see of Malvado the troll. He has vaporized. Don't you agree, Mirasol?"

"It sure looks like it," said Mirasol. "Let's go down to the wheat field and have some more to eat. The disappearance of the troll has made me work up an appetite."

The two flew down to the wheat field, steering clear of the spot where they had last seen the troll. They ate their fill and then moved off to drink pure water from the nearby pond.

No longer hungry or thirsty, they chattered joyfully and flew off toward their castles. As they flew, they saw the gloomy faces of people, some of whom they knew. Were they worried about cultivating their crops in order to pay the stiff taxes the troll demanded? Pachuco wondered.

"How can we tell the citizens of Pacifista that the troll has disappeared and he will not be a threat to them any more?" Pachuco asked. "If we could only make them understand."

They flew on to the Royal Palace. Pachuco didn't know how he would do it, but he had to penetrate the castle and make the Queen understand that the troll would not be coming back.

Pachuco and Mirasol flew to the Royal Palace's servant's quarters where Malvado had said that the former Queen was housed. When they reached the servants' wing, Pachuco saw the soldiers stationed at his mother's door.

"We'll just have to wait for the door to open and rush in," Pachuco said to Mirasol.

The birds hung on to a curtain rod with their talons. Without warning the door to the servants' quarters opened a crack and out ventured Diamante! Pachuco was beside himself.

"Diamante has survived! Diamante has survived!" Pachuco whispered under his breath to Mirasol.

Diamante, a hunting dog, could have rushed the two birds, but instead he cocked his head and stared at them.

"I'm sure he recognizes me," said Pachuco to Mirasol. "He is still the best dog ever."

When Diamante was ready to return to the servants' quarters, the door opened again. The birds flew into the room along with the black Lab.

Pachuco and Mirasol flew in and alighted on the back of the former Queen's chair. She was dozing and did not notice them.

Pachuco squawked, whistled "La Cucaracha," and spoke all the bilingual phrases he knew in his low, raspy voice.

"What could these strange sounds be, and where are they coming from?" she demanded. Pachuco noticed that she had developed a nervous tick and her hair was thinning since he had seen her last.

Pachuco could see a photograph of him, her, and his late father on the table next to her armchair.

"Life under that troll is getting to be more and more unbearable," she sighed. "If only Pachuco were here."

The Amazon wanted more than ever to make her understand that he had returned, and that the troll was no longer a threat to the Kingdom. He could not tolerate seeing his mother, a proud and handsome woman, confined to the servants' quarters of the palace. He could sense how desperate and miserable she was.

Before the Queen could look up and spot Pachuco and Mirasol, Pachuco spied an open window and took off for the outdoors again. Mirasol followed.

"I'm so sorry you couldn't communicate with your mother," said Mirasol. "Let's fly on to my castle. Maybe we'll have better luck with my grandmother."

Pachuco hoped her reunion with her grandmother would not be as heart-wrenching as his visit with the Queen had been.

They flew on to Mirasol's castle. The birds entered the castle through an open window to find the old woman weaving at her loom.

Mirasol exhaled a barely audible breath and lighted on her grandmother's shoulder. Pachuco landed on the edge of the massive loom.

"Look at this," said Lupita. "Two strange birds visiting me as I weave. What a good omen."

Lupita was wistfully singing an ancient Pacifista folk song as she wove fabric for a blanket in muted golds and greens. She hummed and wove with Mirasol clinging to her shoulder until late in the afternoon.

"This is not how the song goes at all," said Mirasol to Pachuco. "She's singing it in a minor key. I've never heard it sound so sad before."

"If only my granddaughter would return," Lupita told the parrots, as she continued weaving, "I would be the happiest person in the Kingdom."

"I'm here, grandmother. Against all odds, I've returned," said Mirasol, but Lupita could not understand her squawking.

Pachuco interrupted the tranquil scene close to sundown. "It's time for us to go watch the sunset, Mirasol," he said gently.

As they departed, Pachuco knew he would long remember Lupita seated at her loom, a smile creeping onto her weathered face, as the Pacifista rainbows began to cast their vivid shadows.

CHAPTER SIXTEEN

The Homecoming

The following morning Mirasol awoke at dawn and called out loudly to Pachuco. He clung to the elm branch next to her with his talons and did not budge.

"Come on, Pachuco, wake up!" she exclaimed. "We have to get an early start today."

"An early start for what?" he asked, as he scratched the spots on his head where his ears were camouflaged by feathers. Then he sneezed several times and began preening.

"Today we are going to the waterfall," said Mirasol matter-of-factly. "You know, the one that's enormous and descends out of a sheer rock cliff. Have you ever seen it, Pachuco?"

"Yes, Mirasol," said Pachuco. "I think I saw it hiking with Diamante the afternoon of the Palace Ball. Each strand of water has a brilliant color, and it roars down a mountain face."

"Yes, that's the one," said Mirasol.

"But why are we going there?" asked Pachuco. "It's on the other side of the Kingdom, and we need to stay close to our castles to see how Pacifista's citizens react to the death of Malvado."

"Pachuco, this is something I know we must do," said Mirasol. "You'll have to trust me on this, the way I trusted you when we were traveling through the wormhole and when you used the red-tail feathers and mistletoe to vaporize Malvado."

"I don't know, Mirasol," said Pachuco. "I have to think about it. It doesn't seem like the day we should go off on a picnic."

"Believe me, Pachuco," said Mirasol, staring at him intently with her black eyes ringed in white feathers. "This will not be a picnic. This is something I've known for days that we have to do. All the time I was in the wormhole I was visualizing the waterfall with its cascading colors, each distinct, each glimmering."

"I knew then we would have to return to the waterfall," continued Mirasol. *"It is important."*

"But why, Mirasol?" asked Pachuco. "It's a beautiful spot, maybe one of the most beautiful in Pacifista, but why do we have to visit it today?"

"I can't explain it in words, Pachuco," said Mirasol. "You'll just have to believe me."

The birds ate their fill once again from the field planted for migratory birds on the Nature Preserve and drank from the nearby pond. Then they took to the air, soaring high over their homeland. Mirasol glided effortlessly over castles as Pachuco breathlessly strained to keep up with her.

"What's the rush, Mirasol?" he asked when he was able to speak.

"I don't know, Pachuco," answered the lovebird. "Something is making me hurry. I am feeling all kinds of strange impulses today.

Maybe returning to Pacifista through the wormhole has set me on edge."

"Relax, Mirasol," said Pachuco. "I have to return the Kingdom to the state it was in before Malvado tried to destroy it, and I have to do it in the form of a Lilac-headed Amazon. Panicking won't help."

At that moment they heard the roar of the waterfall jutting out of the rock cliff. As they descended, sprays of water landed on their feathers making them glisten. Every ten feet of the waterfall was marked in a distinct color, far more alluring than the colors they had seen on Planet Earth, with each strand cascading down to the azure lake below.

Without warning, Mirasol plunged into the whirling waters of the waterfall.

"Mirasol, what are you doing?" shrieked Pachuco. "You will never survive those rushing waters!"

Mirasol batted her wings in the frigid water. She splashed wildly. "Come on in, Pachuco, it's wonderful!" she yelled.

"Mirasol, give me a break here!" Pachuco protested.

At that moment Mirasol could no longer swim and was carried by the current into the depths of the plummeting torrent.

"Where are you, Mirasol?" shrieked Pachuco. "I can't see you any more. There's no way you can survive in there. I'm coming in after you."

Mirasol was barely conscious of Pachuco's green body next to her being pushed along by the rushing water. Pachuco has jumped in after me, she thought. Can he swim? What had she done? Had they been transformed into eggs, traveled down the wormhole, hatched, lived with the old couple, survived attacks by wild creatures, and returned to Pacifista, only to drown? Why had she been so impulsive and jumped into the waterfall?

Mirasol saw Pachuco splash ahead of her in the fomenting water. He's heavier than I am, she thought, he's bound to reach the lake before I will. She could barely breathe in the white water, but she felt strangely exhilarated. She was facing death again but felt sure that this was precisely the place where she and Pachuco should be.

Suddenly the long multi-colored fingers of the waterfall deposited the lovebird into the calming waters of the azure lake. She landed deep underwater. By the time she pushed her way to the surface, she was gasping for breath.

"Pachuco, where are you?" she sputtered. She glanced around the lake and did not see a green parrot with red and lilac markings on his head.

When she had shaken the water from her eyes, she saw Pachuco the King, in his human form, swimming laps in the azure lake. "Pachuco, is that you? I can't believe it!" she exclaimed.

Pachuco stopped swimming and smiled at her. "The magic of the waterfall has transformed me back into my human form. And you are no longer a lovebird. Have you noticed? You are Mirasol, the Princess."

Mirasol glanced down at her body. She had no blue, green, or peach feathers. Instead she had arms, legs, a torso, and a sopping mop of curly, dark hair. She was wearing an old-fashioned bathing suit, the kind she had seen the grandchildren wear when they went to the water slide on Earth. Pachuco, too, wore such a bathing suit.

"This is absolutely *incredible!*" exclaimed Mirasol. "We are human again! The waterfall has transformed us from birds back to humans!"

Though she had sensed the waterfall had magical powers, she had no idea it would transform an Amazon and a lovebird back into a King and a Princess. How this had happened, she would probably never know.

"Your intuition is amazing, Mirasol," said Pachuco. "Thanks to you we are human again."

While Pachuco was still enjoying his morning swim, Mirasol climbed out of the lake. She stepped out onto the shore lined with white pebbles and sat down on a rock. She took several deep breaths. She looked down at her body and gasped. She had just emerged from the lake but was fully dry. She was clothed in the outfit she had worn to the Palace Ball. The dress, not tattered in the least, was floor-length with layers and layers of lace and flower embroidery. Its bodice was fitted; its sleeves were bouffant. Beneath the skirt were her white leather boots that buttoned up the side. They were pure white, not at all muddy. On her head was her cap surrounded by a garland of fresh gardenias, and on her hands were her white silk gloves that extended past her elbows. On her wrist was the corsage of three white roses that her grandmother had given her just before she had left her castle for the Palace Ball.

"Unbelievable!" she called to Pachuco. "Take a look at this!"

Pachuco raised his head above the waters of the lake and looked at her. He let out a whistle.

"More magic, that's for sure," he said.

"Come out and let's see if you're dressed in the clothes you wore to the Ball," said Mirasol.

"I'd like to stay in the water for ten more minutes, Mirasol," said Pachuco. "You can't imagine how much I've missed my morning swim."

Finally he moved towards the shore and pulled himself onto the bank next to her.

As soon as he emerged from the lake he was immediately dry and dressed in the emerald green suit with the black shirt and cummerbund that he had worn to the Palace Ball. On his head was the silk turban with lavender and red highlights.

"That's the fastest I've ever dressed in my life!" Pachuco exclaimed.

"But what kind of shoes are you wearing?" asked Mirasol, when she observed his feet. He was not wearing his ill-fitting black leather dress shoes. Instead he sported a pair of worn sneakers. They fit his feet so perfectly they were like a second skin, and they were so old that she couldn't make out their original color.

Pachuco stared at his sneakers in amazement.

"Look, Mirasol," he said, "I'm wearing my favorite running shoes, the very ones my mother refused to let me wear to the Palace Ball."

Pachuco and Mirasol sat in the sun for a few minutes trying to get over the shock of their transformation to human beings, dressed in their finery for the Ball.

"I guess this means we'll never fly again," said Mirasol moodily. "The sensation of soaring through the air was something I loved, and I'll never forget it for the rest of my life."

"You're right, Mirasol," said Pachuco. "Flying is spectacular. It's something no human can ever comprehend. But I will be happy to return to meals prepared by the chef at the Royal Palace. Maybe I could teach him how to make green chile enchiladas and pastel de chocolate tres leches."

"Maybe," said Mirasol, as her voice trailed off. She doubted that a chef from Pacifista could reproduce foods native to Planet Earth in the next galaxy.

"We've rested long enough," said Pachuco after several minutes. "We have to return to our castles and let the people of Pacifista know that we are back."

"Flying here was easy enough," said Mirasol. "But how do we return to our castles now that we're on foot?"

"There are some hiking paths that Diamante and I took back to the castle," said Pachuco. "I think I can remember the way."

Mirasol followed as Pachuco led her on a bramble-filled hike. They took their time and were careful not to spoil their clothing. At one point Mirasol spotted a large wild cat that would have terrified her had she still been a lovebird. But when she reminded herself she had transformed back into a Princess, she was reassured. In two hours they could see the spire of the Royal Palace.

"Mirasol, I'm going to make contact with my old guards and let them know we have returned," Pachuco said and approached several soldiers on the outskirts of the Palace.

Mirasol saw the astonished faces of the guards. She knew the news of their arrival would spread rapidly throughout Pacifista.

When they arrived at the moat of the Royal Palace, all the drawbridges were open and members of the Royal Court and subjects of Pacifista were gathered in a great throng.

"Is it true?" Mirasol heard the citizens ask. "Have King Pachuco and Princess Mirasol returned? Has the troll been slain?"

She felt like raising her voice and saying, "Yes, yes, yes!" But then she remembered that she was a member of the Court in the Kingdom of Pacifista, and there was Court etiquette to consider. She stood silently next to King Pachuco and waited with him at the front door of the Royal Palace.

Within minutes the door opened widely and out vaulted the black whirlwind that could only be Diamante. He headed for King Pachuco and nearly knocked him over. Mirasol greeted the black Lab as if he were a long-lost friend.

Just then the Queen appeared, and Pachuco left the dog and ran to embrace the Queen who was sobbing gleefully into an embroidered handkerchief.

"Pachuco, my son, you have returned to me! It is truly a glorious day for Pacifista," she exclaimed as she studied him from head to toe. "You seem to be in perfect health. You have no idea how relieved I am."

"The troll transformed us into parrots and sent us to Planet Earth in the next galaxy," explained Pachuco to his mother and to the crowd. "Our voyage was difficult, but rest assured the troll is gone for good. Now we will set about restoring the Kingdom. We have lots of work to do."

"I can't believe the troll is gone, and I have escaped from the servants' quarters. I thought I would end my days there," said the Queen.

The Queen dabbed at her eyes, but Mirasol noticed a radiant smile on her face.

Mirasol looked at all the folks gathered and noticed Lupita edging her way toward the Queen.

"Grandmother, Grandmother, I'm back!" she called loudly.

Mirasol ran and hugged her grandmother, who wept with delight at the sight of her granddaughter.

When Lupita tore herself away from Mirasol's embrace and had the chance to look at her, she said, "How can you still be wearing the outfit we sewed for you for the Palace Ball months ago? It's immaculate," Lupita said. "Even the corsage I made for you is intact. How can this be?"

"I'm not sure," said Mirasol. "There's a lot that I can't explain, but miraculously we're back."

"The Queen and I have become fast friends since you and King Pachuco disappeared," said Lupita. "I visit her every week and bring her homemade bread and soup."

Mirasol found this news surprising, but she supposed that both women comforted each other when faced with the sudden loss of their loved ones. She was glad her grandmother was leaving her castle for more than visits to the produce market.

Mirasol could see the Queen and Pachuco in a huddle near the palace doorway. Finally Pachuco broke away and announced to the crowd, "The Queen and I are proclaiming a week of festivities to celebrate my return with Princess Mirasol from the next galaxy. Every night we will have feasting and dancing for members of the Court and citizens of Pacifista. The festivities will begin tonight at sundown."

A deafening roar rose up from the crowd. They shouted, "Long live the King! Long live the Queen!"

Suddenly Mirasol heard a familiar voice in the crowd. It was her friend Estella who was pushing her way through the throng of people towards Mirasol.

"I knew I'd see you again, Mirasol!" she exclaimed.

"I've missed you, Estella," said Mirasol. "When I was facing the most frightful dangers in the next galaxy, I would think of our hikes and fishing trips. You were always on my mind."

"You seem very different somehow," observed Estella. "Older perhaps, more grown up."

"I feel different," admitted Mirasol, who knew that she could not return to her life as a carefree child in her grandmother's castle after her journey. Mirasol hugged her friend as she and her grandmother left for their castle.

The Princess looked longingly after Pachuco as the two set off. He had become such a large part of her life during their stay in the old couple's kitchen and their travels together.

She convinced her grandmother to attend that evening's celebration. The two set about swiftly sewing a formal dress for Lupita who, despite her visits with the Queen, had not attended a Court function in years. They wove, cut, and fitted her garment, finishing as the sun was setting. While they were working, Mirasol filled Lupita in on the details of her journey to Planet Earth, her transformation into a lovebird, life with the old couple, and the voyage back to Pacifista through the wormhole.

Then the two set out in their wagon for the Royal Palace. When they arrived, they saw tents set up on the Palace grounds. In some of the tents were tantalizing foods such as oysters, crabs, and clams from Pacifista's shoreline; meat from buffalo, elk, and deer that hunters provided from its dense woods; and rich chocolate cakes and puddings made with the beans of cacao from the Kingdom's tropical regions. Other tents housed musical groups, both classical and folk.

Mirasol's first inclination was to run and fill her card for the evening dance program. Instead she and her grandmother waited patiently in the reception line to greet Queen Rosa and King Pachuco. When they reached the head of the line, Pachuco gave Mirasol a broad smile. The Queen kissed Lupita on both cheeks, and then turned toward Mirasol, taking both of her hands in hers.

"Pachuco has told me of your adventures," she said to Mirasol, addressing her loudly so the assembled crowd could hear. "He could never have returned to Pacifista without your ingenuity and intuition."

"You are kind," Mirasol told the Queen. "We both worked very hard to reach the shores of our homeland."

"Kneel down," the Queen instructed Mirasol. "I am going to make you a member of the Inner Circle of the Court, the highest honor that can be bestowed on a woman of Pacifista. You now belong to the highest status in Pacifista's Court. Never has a girl of such tender years received this honor."

Mirasol knelt, and the Queen touched her gently on the right shoulder with her jeweled scepter. Then she placed a heavy gold medallion with the royal shield around the young girl's neck. Lupita looked on, fighting back tears. Pachuco beamed. Even Diamante raced into view, seeming to pant his approval.

The crowd clapped wildly and shouted, "Long live the Princess!"

I guess I've had the adventures I've always dreamed of, thought Mirasol. I wonder what tomorrow will bring.

GLOSSARY

Amiga—Spanish for friend (female)

Birria—Mexican stew made with goat meat

Carnitas—Mexican dish made with pork shoulder roast which is braised, pulled apart, and roasted on high heat

Casita—Spanish for small house

Chile verde—green chile stew made with pork and New Mexican green chiles

Barbacoa—barbeque

Bizcochito—shortbread cookie flavored with anise and cinnamon; New Mexico State cookie

Black hole—an extremely dense object in space formed by the collapse of a star

Bobcat—the most common wildcat in North America, the bobcat is named for its short, bobbed tail. Its coat varies in color from beige to brown fur with spotted or lined markings in dark brown or black.

"*Buenos dias.*"—Spanish for "Good morning."

"*Buenos dias, pajaritos verdes.*"—Spanish for "Good morning, green birds."

"*Calmete*"—Spanish for "Calm down" (to a friend)

Candied tunas—sweetened fruit of the cactus

Carne asada—thin strips of grilled beef often eaten on corn tortillas

Chile rellenos—grilled green chiles stuffed with Mexican cheese and fried

Coyote—a wolf-like mammal with long legs in proportion to a slim body. Unlike wolves, coyotes vocalize and have somewhat larger, less pointed ears and bigger feet.

Dulcita—Mexican candy that come in many varieties (also Mirasol's name on Planet Earth)

Egg tooth—small, sharp bulge on the head of a bird used to break or tear through the egg's surface during hatching

Empanadas de cremas—light, flaky Mexican pastries with a crème filling

"*Ese Pachuco bato loco*, baby, baby, baby boy."—Spanish for "This Pachuco is a crazy guy, baby, baby, baby boy."

Fauna—the animals of a particular region, such as Pacifista

Flora—the plants of a particular region, such as Pacifista

Ghost radiation—radiation that maintains structures of wormholes for a limited time

Great Blue Heron—large wading bird common near shores of open water and wetlands. It is blue-grey overall with black flight feathers and has a gaping beak.

Green chile enchiladas—baked or fried dish made with corn tortillas, cheese, chicken or beef, and green chile

House Sparrow—any of various small birds in the Americas having grayish or brownish plumage

Jalapeño peppers—small, hot green peppers used to make salsa

Kaleidoscope—a tube-shaped optical instrument that is rotated to produce a succession of symmetrical designs by means of mirrors reflecting changing patterns of bits of colored glass; a series of changing phases or events

Lengua—meat of the tongue of an animal

Lilac-headed Amazon Parrot—a medium-sized parrot originating in Mexico that is unreserved, full of personality, good at whistling and talking, and makes a wonderful companion

Lovebird—five-to six-inch bird originating in Africa. Lovebirds are talkative, active, beautiful birds.

Mariachi music—music performed by street bands in Mexico

Meditation—the act or process of reflection achieved by focusing the mind on a phrase or mental image

Menudo—"tripe" stew made from beef stomach lining

Mercado—Mexican market

Milky Way—the galaxy in which Planet Earth is situated

Mistletoe—a shrub with red berries often used as a Christmas decoration in the United States

Moat—a ditch usually filled with water surrounding a castle as protection against assault

Pachuco—Mexican American youths who developed their own subculture during the 1930s and 1940s in the Southwestern United States. They wore distinctive clothing known as "zoot suits" and spoke their own dialect of Mexican Spanish known as Caló.

"*Pachuquito batito*, oh yeah, oh yeah, oh yeah!"—"Little Pachuco, oh yeah, oh yeah, oh yeah!"

Paletas—Mexican popsicles made with tropical fruit like pineapple, coconut, mango, jicama, watermelon, and papaya

Pan mexicano—Mexican bread, light pastry that comes in many varieties and is sold in panaderias (Mexican bakeries)

Pastel de chocolate tres leches—chocolate cake made with three types of cream

Periodic table—arrangement of the elements in a table according to their atomic numbers

Piñatas—hollow cardboard figures covered with colorful crepe paper and filled with candy that falls to the ground when children break them with sticks

Pinto beans—a staple in the Mexican or New Mexican diet that are eaten with rice and corn tortillas to form a complete protein

Pollo en mole—chicken with a spicy Mexican sauce made with chocolate and chile

Posole—soup made with pork, hominy, garlic, onions, chile, cilantro, and broth

Red-Tailed Hawk—raptor with a sharp, hooked beak and rust colored tail. The Mescalero Apaches, a tribe in Southern New Mexico, consider this bird to represent awareness and to be a sign of good luck. They hold the bird's feathers to be sacred.

Roadrunner—a long-legged fast-moving ground bird that is streaked in brown and white and rarely flies. It is the New Mexico state bird.

Salsa—a dip for tortilla chips made with chiles, tomatoes, and onions; also a lively Mexican dance

Talons—claws of birds

Tapestry—a heavy cloth woven with designs or scenes usually hung on walls for decoration and insulation

Tomatillos—a spicy vegetable boiled and sometimes added to salsa

Tortillas—a type of flat bread made with flour or corn

Visible spectrum—distribution of energy emitted by a radiant source that can be seen by the human eye

Warp—the threads running lengthwise in a piece of woven cloth (as opposed to the weft, which runs from side to side)

Western Diamondback Rattlesnake—one of the largest rattlesnake species found throughout New Mexico. Its tail is raccoon-like with its black and white rings.

Wormhole—a worm-shaped structure in space that bridges two universes in which a traveler can move faster than the speed of light. As early as 1935 scientists on Planet Earth, Albert Einstein and Nathan Rosen, understood that the general relativity theory allowed the existence of these "bridges" in space-time. Some scientists on Planet Earth still doubt that wormholes can exist, as they have not solved the problem of discovering enough negative energy to make them viable. Scientists on Pacifista, however, with their superior technology, have resolved this difficulty.

Yellow-throated warblers—small songbirds with plain olive green backs, wings, and tails with yellow throats and upper chests. Males have distinctive black masks.